# Hawaiian Phoenix

## Books and Stories by Ron Mueller

### Brian Oneill Novel

Hawaiian Phoenix
Where They Hide and Reside

### Alex Evercrest Series:

The River Front
The Girl on The Grill
Missing
Maggot
Racist
Votive Candles
Windy City
Country Road
Pool of Blood
Sins of the Daughter
Body Parts
The Skull Collector
The Vanishing

### Taelo Series

The Early Years
The Golden Feather
Journey of Discovery
Dangerous Passage
Condor Clan Slingers
Circumvention
The Journey of Sages
Taelo: Collection

### A Taelo Story:

White Swan and Quiet Pheasant
The Child's Name
Floating Cloud
Quiet Rabbit
Busy Bee
Little Otter & Talking Wren
Broken Spear
Burley Bear & Meadow Flower

### Other books by Ron Mueller

The Door Series:
  The Door
  Delivery
  Journey Beyond
The Savitar Series:
  Journey's End
  Savitar
  Confluence
The Problem Solver Series
  Solutions
  Drug Lords
  Border Crosser

### Single Science Fiction Books:

Current Past and Future
The Event
The Door
Viajante 7

**Imagination** by Courtney Huynh and Chloe Parker

# Hawaiian Phoenix
### By: *Ron Mueller*

Around the World Publishing LLC
4914 Cooper Road Suite 144
Cincinnati, Ohio 45242-9998



## Hawaiian Phoenix


ISBN 13: 978-1-68223-986-5
ISBN 10: 1-68223-986-1

Distributed by Ingram
Model Picture by: CURA photography @ShutterStock
Hawaii Picture by: Skvoor @ShutterStock
Phoenix Picture by: Weerchai Dhamfu @ShutterStock
Cover Design by: Ron Mueller

Ron Mueller

## <u>Table of Content</u>

Ron Mueller

## **Chapter 1: Pukalani "The window of heaven"**

She was dying.  She was only twenty-nine, but she had been given the news that at the most she had about three months to live.

She was single.  She had a six-year-old son.  Her treasure in life but she was dying and had no one that would take care of him.

Her parents had disowned her when she graduated from high school, and they had booted her out of the house and wished her luck.

It was not long after that both of them were killed in a car accident.  Being brought up by them had not been easy.  They both drank too much and spent most of each weekend watching some sports game while they argued about the players as they drank and called in bets to a bookie.  They were always short on money and skimped on food but made sure they had their case of beer ready for when they watched the games.

She had made the school's cheerleading squad and had enjoyed being sought after by a slew of high school boys. It was the same week that she graduated when she was kicked out of the house where she had grown up.

Her parents gave her two hundred dollars and wished her good luck. They both told her to get a job and fend for herself. It turned out that her good looks were the single thing that provided a quick and easy income. She moved in with a friend but realized that the cold winters of the northwest were not for her.

She decided to move to Hawaii and ended up in Maui. Maui was a paradise for her. The balmy weather, the miles of beaches, and the pace of life seemed to calm her soul. It was easy to meet eager young men that were willing to contribute to her financial well-being.

She did not know who had delivered her death sentence to her, but she knew that it was her fault for making money on her back.

That was how Brian, who had just turned six that week, was conceived. The drugs she had been on had almost killed him. He was born addicted and had to be slowly weaned from the drugs that her body had transferred to him. When she realized that she was responsible for the pain and agony that her crying baby seemed to be going through, she went cold turkey.

# Hawaiian Phoenix

When he turned three, he had asked about his father, and she had told him that he had been given to her by a stork.

In fact, his tall, dashing, and big spending father had swept her off her feet but for him she was just a toy that he enjoyed during his Hawaiian vacation.

She was sure that his father was very well to do because she had written to him and let him know that he had a son with her. His response had been to set up a childcare support trust, dutifully put in money each month since Brian's birth and made her its trustee. He wished her good luck and that she should not interfere with his personal life in the future.

She had been surprised at his generosity but was surprised at his lack of interest in his son. She had consciously guarded the trust. She knew her weakness was the use of a variety of drugs, and therefore she did not trust herself to keep her hands out of the money pot, so she had transferred the management of the trust to a professional money management group. It had been a smart move because there had been times when she wanted to raid the fund so that she could get her next fix.

When she was diagnosed with a terminal illness, she had no idea what she was going to do with Brian. She had never been a church goer. She walked into a small church that had always caught her eye. It had a steeple and, on the hour, regularly rang a bell. She had walked by it almost every day and had always wondered what it would be like to be a churchgoer. She entered and was greeted by a nun who welcomed her.

The nun did not seem much older than herself, but it was clear to Alec that the nun had a very different take on life than she did.  Her smile seemed to open a door to a warm, sunny world.

After sharing the fact that she was dying and had a young son and was trying to figure out how he could be raised once she passed on.

The nun went to a small office and returned with the number of a local foster care agency.  She suggested that Alec call them to see how they might help.

The conversation then turned to how the church might help her.  She thanked the nun for her concern but said that she really did not believe in an afterlife and smiled and added that if there was one, she would most likely be facing an angel that had horns.

The nun shook her head and went over to the podium and returned with a rosery and a small booklet that accompanied it. She commented that the rosary provided a way for a person to talk to those above and might provide comfort in the coming days.  She suggested one prayer might be the most useful to a non-believer.

"Our Father, who art in heaven, hallowed be Thy name; Thy kingdom come; Thy will be done on earth as it is in heaven. Give us this day our daily bread; and forgive us our trespasses as we forgive those who trespass against us; and lead us not into temptation, but deliver us from evil, Amen."

# Hawaiian Phoenix

She invited Alec to return on Sunday.  She added that it was never too late to become a believer.

Shortly after walking out of the church, Alec made the call to the foster care agency.  She was invited to see the home that they called Pukalani where the children resided and how they were treated.  The person on the other end suggested that Alec take her son to get an evaluation by a counselor that worked with the foster care agency.

Alec arranged for the evaluation.

She decided to go and see the foster home on her own and if she decided to put Brian into the facility, she would then take him there and see what he thought of the place.

As she drove to the facility she could see the islands of Lanai, Kaho'olawe and the Molokini crater.  The view was majestic as the darker blue green waters of the ocean contrasted against the lighter blue of the clear sky.  She stopped in the uphill drive that led to the home that she was coming to see and stood by her car for a moment looking out to the horizon.  The view seemed to embrace her and warm her soul.  She hoped Pukalani and the people running it would match the impressive view.  She felt that it would be a great place for Brian to grow up.

She drove the rest of the way up the driveway into a level courtyard that was bordered with low purple flowers providing a contrast to the light green of the two-foot high neatly trimmed hedge.  Beyond the hedge she could see a playground and then what appeared to be a well-tended garden.

The courtyard had parking for four cars and had a basketball hoop at one end. It was clear to her that the owners of this facility seemed oriented towards children.

The house had a surround glassed in veranda that looked out on the courtyard and also provided a view across to the islands. It seemed like a wonderful place.

Now she was hoping to get the same impression of the folks running the place as she had so far had of the environment.

The lady that met her seemed to be only a few years older than she was. She introduced herself as Kaia and invited her in and was led to a kitchen table that had a pot of hot water and two cups.

She accepted a cup of tea as she sat down. She was then asked about her request to place her son in the home.

Alec began by sharing the fact that she was terminally ill and had been told she had only about one month left. She said she was trying to place her son in a home where he would be well taken care of. She shared that she had reviewed her options and as a resident of Hawaii she was eligible to place her son into a registered home and social security would cover the expense.

She had taken Brian to the phycologist that Kaia had suggested, and he was interviewed by her. She had cleared him as a normal youngster that was doing well in second grade.

She added that her son had a trust fund that was managed by professional money managers that was intended to cover emergencies and then be available for his continuing education.

Alec then asked if Kaia was going to accept Brian.

Kaia asked about potential relatives that might take Brian in.

Alec shared that her parents were both killed in a car accident, and she did not know any other members in the family.

Kaia asked the phycologist's name that had evaluated Brian.

Alec responded that it was Dr. Marian Nelson.

Kaia nodded and said that Marian and she were friends and if she had cleared Brian then she would accept him into Pukalani. She added that Brian would be the only child with green eyes and blond hair and that all the other children were native Hawaiians that were there temporarily and slated to be returned to their parents.

She asked if Alec had any concerns if a Hawaiian family were to adopt him.

Alec shook her head and said that she had none if the family was cleared for the adoption, and she smiled and said that she would have no way to object unless there was some sort of miracle.

Kaia asked if there was a way for them to meet for lunch so that Brian could meet her and her husband before he came to live with them.

Alec said that she thought that would be a good idea and asked where they should have lunch.

Kaia suggested a pizza place in Paia and asked if they could do a dinner instead of lunch so both she and her husband could do it after working hours.  Then afterwards they could take a walk along the beach.

Alec left with the feeling that she had found the perfect place for Brian.

Late the next afternoon she arrived at the restaurant.  Brian loved the pizza and afterwards on the beach he and Kaia's husband, Anakoni, who asked to be called Koni, spent time passing a football back and forth.

Alec felt that finding Brian a good home with what seemed like good people was one of the better things she had done.  She felt the pressure she had been letting build up dissipate.

She returned to the church and let the young nun know that her recommendation had worked out and let her know the home that Brian was going to live in.

In the following week she began to feel her body shutting down.  She drove Brian to his new home and told him that was where he would now be living.  She gave him a hug as he began to cry and told him to always remember that he was her treasure and that she would always love him.

She had told him that she was dying before taking him up to Pukalani, and they had cried together.  It was an extremely emotional moment and she appreciated how both Kaia and Koni stood back to let her have her last moments with her son.

# Hawaiian Phoenix

She had closed all her worldly concerns. One of the last things had been to transfer her car title to Kaia. Kaia drove her to the hospice that she had selected and dropped her off. In less than a week, Alec took her last breath. It had been a swift, painless departure.

When she died, she had no way of knowing how Brian would grow both in body and in spirit and that he would be like a phoenix rising from the ashes. He would become very successful, find his soul mate, and make a financial fortune while putting cheating billionaires in prison. Whether she was looking down or looking up she would see that she had been the ashes from which spread his wings and rose.

There were only four people at her funeral ceremony: Kaia, Koni, Brian, and Dr. Marian Nelson.

Marian had established a close relationship with Brian and sat holding his hand during the ceremony. Alec had been cremated and the ceremony consisted of a brief biography and then a series of pictures that Alec had selected of her and Brian that she had cherished.

Marian wiped the tears from her eyes and those from Brian. She was heartbroken by seeing him crying. She had developed an instant bond with him when she had evaluated him for the state to ensure that he would fit in a foster home. He was a bright, happy child that seemed to be very intelligent. He was definitely as Irish as they came. He had green eyes, blond hair with a tinge of red and was slender and tall for his age.

After the ceremony they all went for a long walk along the beach.  Then Kaia sat in the back seat with Brian and Koni drove up to their home.  It was the home that would for the next decade be home for a young boy that would end up calling both of them Makuahine and Makuakane.

He would become a young man of Irish American descent that was to grow up fluent in the traditional Hawaiian culture and language.  He would be the person that understood the value of family.

## **<u>Chapter 2: Makuas, His Parents</u>**

Kaia sat on the veranda and watched Koni playing basketball with Brian.  She and Koni had discussed adopting Brian but had decided not to take a chance of getting rejected.  Instead, they had focused on raising him in a manner that they would have raised their own child.  They had found out that she was not able to conceive so Brian filled the void that would otherwise have existed.  Brian was a very intelligent boy and was always at the head of the classes he was in.  He was also a very kindhearted person and often volunteered to help his classmates with schoolwork and she found out that for an entire school year he shared the lunch she sent with him with a young girl whose parents were on the down and out.

It had been six years since his mother had passed.  He had a picture of her hanging on the wall with the dried palm leaf that had been part of her ceremony.  A large, framed picture of her and Koni with their arms around him was on his bedside table. Brian had written Makuahine, Makuakane and Keikikāne in beautiful calligraphic lettering.

She had watched him sitting at the kitchen table practicing on paper until he had mastered getting the names done with no errors and then he had finally put the Hawaiian names for mother, son, and father under each of their pictures.

That was the day that she and Koni had celebrated the fact that they had made the right decision in embracing Brian as their own.

He had become a talented basketball player as well as a football player.  He had played soccer for several years and was a top goalkeeper for the teams he had played on.  His height, balance and speed gave him an advantage in each of those sports.

His looks attracted many young ladies, but he did not seem interested in having anything but friends.  He was not into the girlfriend thing, but he had several girls that were his friends.  He also had several boys with whom he buddied around.  The group of mixed gender friends often went out surfing and sailboarding.

She and Koni would always go with him and his friends to ensure that everyone wore the appropriate safety gear.  They were teased about being overprotective of their haole, or white boy.  That did not bother either of them.  They loved their haole and embraced him as their own.

They did everything together from planting and tending the garden, to cooking and grilling as well as attending sporting events, going to plays and concerts to surfing together.  The three enjoyed each other and were constantly talking and laughing together.

They were looking forward to Brian's high school years, but they had already talked about the fact that those years were going to pass too quickly.  They had promised each other that they were going to be parents that stayed close to their only child.

The high school years went by in a blur.  Brian earned a letter in three sports.  He was on the student council.  He was a freelance contributor to the school paper.  But most importantly he was one of the top five students in his graduating class.  He had applied to multiple schools and had received scholarship offers to several colleges.

He did not get an offer from the school that he had his mind set on, so he chose to go to the University of Hawai'i Maui College.  He figured he would take the basics and continue to try to get into the University College Dublin (UCD), in Belfield Ireland.  He shared the fact that he was going to continue to apply to both UCD and to the University of Oxford.

He admitted that he was curious about what his paternal side did and to find out whether he had any other half siblings.

He then surprised both of them and said that he planned to split his trust with the two of them so they would have the means to travel to see him whenever they desired.  He pointed out that visiting him during his undergraduate years in Ireland would allow them to see Europe as well.

She and Koni had regularly taken Brian to meet with the financial analyst that was the executor of the trust and had wisely managed it to the point that when Brian graduated, and he became the executor it had three hundred thousand dollars in it.

They declined his offer and said that he should continue to grow the fund so that it would not only cover his education but would put him on the road to financial stability.

He ended up spending one year going to school on Maui before he was accepted by UCD who offered him a full scholarship and a stipend if he participated with the local police as part of his education while he went to the university.

They all celebrated his acceptance and agreed to visit the university together.  He had gotten a place in the UCD resident hall.  So, his expenses would easily fit the budget that he was planning to follow.  He would not have to pay the thirty thousand dollars a year that foreign students normally paid.  He admitted that it gave him great relief not to have to spend the money in his trust fund.

He suggested they go early and take a tour of Ireland and that they all spy together on what his biological father did and how rich he might be.  He said that other than learning about his father he did not plan to contact him.

They had agreed to the tour and said that they planned to stay out of the spy game.  They would spend that time walking the Irish countryside.

He smiled and said that he did not plan to spend too much time at his spy game either, but he wanted to learn why his biological father had been willing to be generous with his child support but had not wanted to learn more about the person that he had brought into the world.

Kaia and Koni both said that they would look forward to touring Ireland with him and said that they would also like to visit The Netherlands and Denmark on the trip.

Brian arrived in Ireland three days before both of his parents. He checked in with the UCD admissions office and got a room assignment. Shortly after getting all his things into his room, he went on his spying mission. He had done an online search and had found information on his biological father. It turned out that he was a very well-known lawyer known for taking on hard cases and winning. He was also known to be a generous contributor to food relief and other charitable organizations. Brian concluded that his biological father was a good man.

He waited outside of the office where his father worked but soon realized that one of the cars that had driven into the basement garage had most likely held his father. He spent the day touring the city and then in the late afternoon had gone to his father's home address. This turned out to be an address that led him to a point that overlooked a tree lined glen that had a herd of sheep, a few cows, a huge castle like home and at least a half mile long driveway.

He stood outside of the cab that he had hired and commented at the serene and peaceful scene of the glen.  He was again disappointed by the fact that his spying was not going the way he had envisioned.

He had determined that his biological father was indeed well to do, seemed to be a person of high character and lived with his family on an inspiring piece of land.

He decided that he would have to take a different approach to learning more about his biological father.

He returned to the city and decided that it was time to switch his focus to spending time with the two people he considered his parents.  He set up a tour of the city and arranged for a tour of UCD.  He then spent the rest of the day doing his own exploring of his new university.

## **Chapter 3: Reflection**

The vacation with Kaia and Koni turned out to be an amazing and wonderful time.  Brian arranged for a car and driver to go for a road trip around the Wild Atlantic Way.  They started out in Dublin and headed toward Cork then to Galway on to Sligo and then back to Dublin.  He booked hotels in each to those cities.

It was an epic road trip with spellbinding scenery of the Irish coastline in and around Sligo, Galway, and Cork.

They skipped the crowd favorites like the Cliffs of Moher and instead hit up the Fanad Head in Donegal.  Climbed up the seventy-six stairs by Fanad Head Lighthouse to get the most breathtaking view of the wild Atlantic Ocean.

They took a detour out of Cork and went on an eat your way around Kinsale day outing before heading north to Galway.

Kinsale was originally a Norman fishing port meaning "Head of the Sea," it was known as the gourmet capital of Ireland.  It had excellent restaurants that highlighted local food producers and artisans.

They were enthralled by the colorful buildings and the impressive, fortified walls of the spectacular yet Charles Fort from which they had a stellar view of the harbor and countryside.

They then back tracked and went on to Galway where they stayed overnight.

The next day they went on to Sligo by way of Castlebar where they stopped for lunch.

The round trip took them six days.

They then flew to Amsterdam and took a car tour of the city and a riverboat day trip the following day.

They went on to Copenhagen, Denmark and had toured the yellow blooming mustard field countryside and then took a tour boat across to Malmo, Sweden and spent the afternoon there.

It was a true memory making trip for the three of them.  He felt closer than ever to them.  He knew that they would forever be the two he called his mother and father.

His school session had started the day after he returned.  It had been a whirlwind experience that he would not forget.

Brian walked along the Sandymount beach walking trail.  He sat down on a bench and began to reflect on his life as he watched the gentle waves wash in.  A small stick floating on the water caught his eye and he thought about the years that had floated serenely by during his life.  The stick was pushed forward a small distance and then slid down into the trough behind the wave.  Each wave was slowly bringing the stick to shore.  It made him think about his life on Maui.

# Hawaiian Phoenix

He had a biological mother that had died young but who for all her faults had made sure that he was in a home where he would be well taken care of.

He had a biological father that was very well to do and had been financially generous but who had not shown any interest in him as a person.

He had two wonderful people that he called Makuahine, mother and Makuakane, father who had raised him and given him the values to live by. The one value he had embedded in his mind was to treat others as he wished to be treated.

He had a phycologist, who was a close friend to Kaia who he called Anakē, Aunt, who had molded his mind to be self-aware and self-challenging.

He had an educational experience that had allowed him to grow and develop his mind. That same experience had supported his athleticism. He had excelled in football, basketball, and soccer. He smiled as he thought about the fact that he had been a jock but a quiet and bashful one. He made many friends of both sexes, but he never clicked with any of the young women that surrounded him. He had been active on the stage and had appeared in several plays. He was also an independent contributor to the school paper. His articles normally featured the charitable events that various clubs sponsored.

He had also helped Kaia and Kori in managing the home they provided for a variety of young children.

He watched a small nut floating on a wave as it went by and smiled and thought that he was a little like the nut.  He was in a world that held a great deal of potential for him, and he was now going to be able to pursue almost any career that he desired.  He had latched on to being in law enforcement.  Very much like the nut he was being swept along on the long waves of life to some place that he had yet to learn about.

He was not interested in the run of the mill law enforcement.  He was interested in catching those who chose to take advantage of the law and step on the small people that made up the bulk of the population.  The nut was being taken for a ride on the sea.  He was sure that his own life might end up very much that way.  It could turn out to be a ride to the sea of turbulence and trouble, but he planned to ride life's waves like a world class surfer.

The toll of a nearby church announced that it was twelve.

Brian decided that a trip to some downtown eatery was next on his agenda.  He jogged back to his room where he changed into some sports clothes before heading out to eat.

He had purchased a new electric assist bike to ride, that he kept in the bike storage room of the building.  He took it out and headed to the restaurant he had in mind.

It was a short ride, and he was just finishing locking his bike to the bike rack when he looked across the street and recognized the person walking along with a very good looking blond, blue-eyed woman with three children laughing and joking with each other as they followed.

# Hawaiian Phoenix

He kept his bike helmet on and stayed on his knees as he observed them entering the restaurant across from the one, he was getting ready to enter.

He went into the restaurant and chose a table by the window that gave him a view across the street. He took his time in placing the order and ate slowly. He wanted to get a good view of the family when they left the restaurant.

He paid for his lunch but sat and nursed his iced tea waiting for his biological father to exit the restaurant. When the family exited the restaurant, he felt as if he were looking at an older version of himself. There was no doubt who he was looking at. The two boys looked different than their father and he figured that the youngest, a girl, was going to look exactly like her mother. It was clear that they seemed like a happy family.

He walked out of the restaurant, put on his bike helmet, and got his bike. He walked down the street opposite the family. They walked back to a sleek, red, convertible, Lamborghini and all got in and drove off.

He stood for a moment looking down the street and then got on his bike and headed for the river. He had achieved what he had sought to learn about his father, but it left him less than fulfilled. He did not feel like what he had expected.

He thought again about the two people that he now considered his real parents and smiled because they had provided him with the love and warmth that had let him grow up with a self-confidence that he knew would carry him throughout life.

They would draw him back from Ireland to Hawaii and the land that he loved.

He knew that now he could focus on his education and getting through the University. He was more than eager to get on with the goal of seeking out the big bad guys.

During school breaks he would return to Hawaii and relax in the land he called home. He would spend as much time as possible surfing, walking the beaches but also participating in the food kitchen where over the years he had become a regular.

It was a small island and he liked making his way around to all the nooks and crannies. He had several good high school friends who he went out with on many of the outings.

He had a few dates, but they had not gone beyond the second date. He had not felt the connection on any of his dates, so he had decided to wait until he felt the pull. He figured that somewhere along the line it would happen, and he was allowing time to play out the romance in him on its own timeline.

The family took vacation trips to Japan, Thailand, and took a cruise along the Canadian coast up to Alaska.

The Alaskan cruise was on a smaller ship that had only a couple of hundred people on it. He really enjoyed the time that the three of them spent with each other on guided tours on shore that took them to a glacier. Along the way they saw moose, several large bears, and some wolves. The panoramic view and the cracking sounds of the glacier greatly impressed them.

They all claimed to have gained ten pounds eating the lunches and dinners that went from salmon to deer meat prepared by a chef the seemed to only prepare award-winning meals.

At BCD he focused on staying at the top of his class. This meant many hours of study. He did his studying in a variety of places such as the beach shore, or the pub that he enjoyed, or the school library, even sitting on the bench in front of his dorm.

The time seemed to both crawl and then race forward. His trips home were great breaks that raced by and on return to school the time was in the crawl mode but as the school year progressed time there began to race.

He did not rank in the top ten, but he was number eleven in his class. He asked several of his favorite professors to give him letters of recommendation. He gave them a draft of the recommendation letter and asked them to send their edited version to Standford University and he provided an addressed and stamped envelope to use.

He had achieved the goal of keeping his grades as close to the top as possible and when he applied to Stanford University he was accepted into their graduate program.

He let Kaia and Anakoni know about the acceptance and that he was coming home to celebrate with them, and they should pick the restaurant of their choice.

The reply was that they would celebrate with all his friends on the veranda of their house.

He got a congratulating message from Marian, the person he now called Aunt, congratulating him on his great achievement. She pointed out the significant journey that he had already taken and that the journey ahead seemed to be as challenging.

Stanford Campus was the opposite in size and distances between buildings as the ones on BCD. His bicycle was indispensable. Periodically on the days that he had the fewest books to carry he would jog between the buildings that he needed to get to. He did a lot of jogging on the weekends that allowed him to enjoy the expanse that was the Stanford campus.

Like all college campuses, there was a variety of eating, drinking and partying establishments just outside of the campus area.

The Stanford program took him a year and a half. It was definitely on the whirl wind end of the spectrum. He felt that he was behind for the entire time, but he did exceedingly well and this time he was in the top ten of his class.

He was number three.

He then spent nine months working to get his law degree. That effort was as difficult and dry as it could be. He knew then that he really did not want to actually practice law. He wanted to be in law enforcement but on a much more practical level. He wanted to catch the sophisticated, high roller thief that was bending the law to his advantage.

He was content with letting those who enjoyed practicing law in the courtroom prosecute the people he intended to hand over to them.

He finally felt ready to pursue his goal.

He moved back to Maui and rented a home close to the coast above the Blue Golf course.  He set up his home office and began his investigation online.

He had no clue how he was going to get started.  He spent hours perusing the business news online looking for some individual that seemed to raise a red flag for him.

An article that featured a city landlord, Henry Ludley Winchester II, that was buying older buildings and evicting the current tenants so he could convert the building to upper end condo's that he could lease to wealthy young professionals caught his eye.

He did an online search on the history of Henry and learned that he was a billionaire that had made his money by purchasing older apartment buildings in locations that would attract young business professionals and converting them into condos.  This was done in an entirely legal way.  However, the law was one that had been written and sponsored by the real estate agents and politicians that were influenced by him and other wealthy individuals like him.

His research led him to believe that Henry had done some very shady deals that were in the grey area of the law. He began to look more closely at the deals that had been made.

Ron Mueller


26

## **<u>Chapter 4: Wealth</u>**

He felt like he was being watched but did not see anyone suspicious.  He led the way to his Lamborghini and after everyone was in, he headed back to the house.  They were planning to relax and lounge around the pool, play some tennis, and do some putting.

Something had triggered his mind and now he was into one of his journeys.  This time for some reason it took him back to one of his first vacations as a young graduate where he had gone to Hawaii on his own.  It was a vacation that had cost him more than he anticipated.  He had met a very beautiful young woman that he later realized was a prostitute.  He had slept with her almost every night while he was in Hawaii.  He had enjoyed every moment with her, but he had no long-term interest in her.

He returned to Ireland and began his career.  His family connections gave him a clear advantage in setting up his realty business and soon he was very well to do and connected at every business and political level.

He soon realized that his wealth was actually a hindrance for his social life.  There was no shortage of women willing to go out with him.  However, they were usually more interested in his wealth than anything else.

He actually stopped dating until one of his friends let him know that he had the perfect woman for him.

It was at this time when his Hawaiian vacation came back into his life.  The woman he had spent two weeks in bed with let him know that he was the father to a beautiful baby boy.  The letter she had sent included a picture of the baby and then another of the boy when he was three.  He had no doubt that he was the father.

He had his lawyer set up a trust and fund it with a starting forty thousand dollars with instructions to pay one thousand dollars a month into the trust until the boy reached the age of eighteen.  He hoped to keep what was in Hawaii, in Hawaii.  He did not need the complication in his life in Ireland.

The woman his friend had set him up with was now sitting on a raft in the middle of the pool.  She was the person that had penetrated his shield and was the mother of his three children.  They were three wonderful children that warmed his heart and had provided endless days of joy.

He wondered about his first child. It had been well beyond twenty years ago. He should be in his late twenties. He wondered if he had used the trust fund to get an education. He hoped so. He decided that he wanted to find out more about that situation.

Four years passed before he returned to that thought. He was watching his daughter celebrate her thirteenth birthday when once again he thought about his son in Hawaii. He called the investigator he used and asked him to look into what that son was doing.

It took several weeks and when he read the initial report, he was shocked. His son had attended University College Dublin (UCD), in Belfield Ireland. He had graduated near the top of his class.

So, he had been that close for several years and had not contacted him. He was sure that his son had observed him. He wondered why he had not made contact.

The next surprise was that his son had attended Stanford where he got his master's degree. Then he had gone on to get his law degree and license.

He was more surprised to find out that his son was not pursuing the normal path as a lawyer but pursuing the ultra-rich who had skirted the law.

It became clear that his son had made Hawaii his home.

Rory was saddened to learn that his son's mother had died shortly after he had set up the trust fund but pleased that the people that had taken him in had taken good care of him and had raised him to the point that he considered them his mother and father.

He was also pleased that it appeared that his son was an astute handler of his money. He had just recently graduated and gone into business, but he already owned three rental properties plus had purchased a new home overlooking a golf course. It was more than most people his age would have accomplished.

His detective had also summarized the three legal cases that his son was pursuing against the one person that he had singled out.

There was one case in Mississippi that was based on the illegality of stealing an apartment building from a Black individual. He had manipulated the property deed so that a third party ended up as the legal owner and the money promised to the actual owner was diverted to an account that ended up being managed by the person doing the buying.

This Rory knew was pure thievery but the legal case that his son brought against the individual was about avoiding the taxes associated with the purchase and improvement of the property. He admired the fact his son had realized that the stealing of the property was beyond the time of viability, but tax avoidance was not. It was a very good strategy.

The case in Kentucky was similar but the RICO statue had been invoked and it allowed the various Mafia connections and the steal in Mississippi to be brought up in state court and made very public.  This would help the case in Mississippi.  The folks in Kentucky had been convinced to change their case to imply illegal manipulation by a variety of shady people that resulted in them losing control of their property.  Rory recognized the power of this approach.

Both of these cases requested that the property be returned to the original owner.

The owner in Mississippi had passed away but his relatives had eagerly agreed to them gaining the rights to the property.

The folks in Kentucky were also amenable to the financial arrangement that stipulated they pay for the lawyer's fees and seven percent to him.

Rory saw immediately that the strategy in the two cases was not to imprison the rich individual but to make him pay real money for his misdeeds.

He was glad that he personally had never pursued such a low-level way to make money.  He would hate for his son to single him out in such a manner.

The third case that was based in California had a more interesting twist.  Henry Winchester II lived next door to a Judge in Beverly Hills.  This neighborly relationship had been taken advantage of by having the judge link him up to another friend judge.

That judge presided over the case where the apartment building acquired in a shady way was being contested. Henry had lavishly treated the judge to gifts and a substantial political donation. In return he got the case against him thrown out.

Rory's son had sued him in civil court for damages of ten million dollars. There was no time limit in civil court so the case could be used to get the property back.

The detective doing the reporting let him know that all three cases were being handled separately but all had top lawyers handling the cases. Rory figured that the three lawyers and Brian were in close communication because each case was scheduled to allow them to use the outcome of the previous one to help them in the subsequent case.

Rory recognized and admired the sharp strategy being deployed.

His detective had also made the point that Brian was doing in-depth, on-site investigation to ensure the lawyers had the most detailed and pertinent information. He also shared the fact that an unknown individual had visited the judge in the Mississippi trial, and they had gone to a bar where he had a meeting with Henry Winchester II. The information seemed make Henry upset because he slammed his hand down on the bar where he was sitting.

Brian was indeed on site getting the detailed paper records that had never transferred into a computer system.  He went to the county courthouse where the hotel in Mississippi was located.  He found the deed for the hotel and the name of the final owner.  Additional research of the name led to the fact the name was a pseudo name for Henry Winchester II.  This clearly showed the fact that the property was stolen.

Brian wanted the fact of the steal put into the documents that would be reviewed by the judge.  He was not seeking punishment for the steal but was seeking that the deed be returned to the rightful owners.  He also wanted financial recompense for ten years of lost income and financial growth that the family had lost.

There was no jury.  It had been Henry's choice not to have it be a trial by jury, but a settlement determined by the judge.  He had privately hoped to be able to sway the judge with gifts.

Brian figured that Henry would most likely try to buy the judge off.  He had done his own evaluation of the judge and had decided that he was dealing with a true, hardline, honest judge that had a reputation of being hard but fair to the guilty.

The paperwork was submitted to the judge and Brian more or less held his breath waiting for the judge to review the detailed paperwork.

Three days later he was sitting with his prosecuting lawyer and Henry was sitting at the defense desk with his lawyer when the judge entered and asked everyone to rise.

He then clearly read his decision. He announced that he had decided that the building rightfully belonged to the heirs of the person who had been cheated out of his property. Additionally, he was levying a five-million-dollar penalty for lost income. Finally, he was sentencing Henry Winchester II to six years in prison for tax evasion on that property.

The silence from the defense table was thundering.

Brian wanted to jump up and down in celebration. The Judge had read, understood, and agreed with the entire document that his lawyers had presented.

The family that had been cheated did what Brian wanted to do, they shrieked, hollered, and danced.

The judge brought down his gavel and declared the case closed.

He ordered the court police to hand cuff and take their prisoner out and book him.

Brian had met with the family multiple times. They had agreed with the trial but said that they had little hope of a positive outcome. Now they surrounded him, hugged him, and said that he should get ten times what he had said he was charging.

He was satisfied with the seven percent of market value. He had worked with the lawyers to limit them to seven percent as well. He had sweetened the deal for the lawyers by allocating forty percent of his seven percent to them as a bonus if they won the case. This left him with approximately three million dollars for each case in Mississippi and Kentucky.

The Kentucky case had a twist in it because they had chosen to use the Racketeer Influenced and Corrupt Organizations Act (RICO) as the basis of moving the case into the federal jurisdiction.

Brian had been able to link several mafia figures with interactions with Henry Winchester II. He had identified at least two mafia figures that had interacted with Henry and placed them at the Kentucky site at the time that the crime was committed. He had hired lawyers that were familiar with this type of case, and they had done wonders in making sure there would be no escape.

The judge read the guilty verdict and sentence Henry to the minimum of fifteen years. The sentence was to begin at the end of the sentence set down in the Mississippi case.

He then returned the property to its rightful owner.

Once again, the owner and his family celebrated the event and swarmed the defense table. They were jubilant and wanted to celebrate with him.

He thanked them but said that he had one more case on the west coast that he had to see to, to ensure that Henry received all the was due him.

After congratulating his lawyers, he made his way to the airport to catch his flight to LA.

Pasadena was a short drive from the airport.  He had rented a room at the Hilton and before retiring he decided to drive to see Henry's home.  He wanted to see the neighborhood and get a feel for the environment.

It was a nice neighborhood but there was nothing extravagant about it.  Large oak and maple trees lined the street and a long flower and hedge lined retaining wall bordered the raised yards of the houses.  The garage for most of the homes was accessed from the street behind the houses.  The houses were at least one hundred years old.  It was a place where one could safely raise a family.  It seemed out of character for the billionaire he was successfully prosecuting.

The trial was of a different nature.  It was not a money scam but one of bribing the judge with a political donation.  This was a case where the judge was about to lose his license to practice law and to be removed from the bench.  Henry faced a minimum sentence of twenty years.  If found guilty all together he would be in prison for the rest of his life.

The trial proceeded rapidly.  Henry received the twenty years and was immediately escorted out of the court room.

The judge that had originally given Henry the green light in the swindle of the property was barred from practicing law and the stolen property was returned to its rightful owner.

Brian tallied up the money he had made.  Roughly seven percent of four hundred million or twenty-eight million.  But he had promised forty percent of his share to the lawyers as a bonus for winning their cases, which left him with sixteen million.  He thought about that figure and wondered what he would do with so much money.  He decided that he would set up some sort of philanthropic organization to help less fortunate people.

It was time to return to Hawaii and enjoy watching the sunset from his home.

Ron Mueller

38

## **<u>Chapter 5: Soul Mate</u>**

He entered his house, went to the living room window, and looked out at the lights of the hotels and condos below him. The black beyond was the ocean and the dark night sky. There was no moon visible.

He stood for a few minutes and decided that it was time for him to get some rest. It had been a grueling month of many hours and tense moments. He was looking forward to the weekend and to taking a slow relaxing walk on the beach.

He planned to visit his parents the next day and let them know that he was back for the foreseeable future and would be working from home. He was sure they would be surprised at how much money he had made in such a short time. When he had told them he was not going to be a courtroom lawyer they had wondered how he was going to make a living.

He almost felt that he was somewhat of a Robin Hood but in his case, he was stealing from the rich crooks and would give back to the needy.

The following morning, he called home and talked to Kaia who insisted he come up for lunch.  He agreed to do so and said that he wanted to come back to his house early so he could walk on the beach to relieve some of the stress he had accumulated during the trials that had just occurred.

Later when he entered the kitchen, he saw that lunch was large enough to feed a small army.  Kaia had prepared a roast duck, asparagus and purple sweet potatoes and a mixed green salad.

He was glad he was planning a long walk on the beach.

Aunt Marian was also at lunch, and she had brought the dessert.

It was a very enjoyable, chatty lunch and everyone was glad that he was home.

He waited until the dessert made up of a strawberry rhubarb pie dessert with a scoop of vanilla was at the table.  He sipped his coffee and said that he had some amazing news to share but he wanted to finish his dessert first.  Once he saw that everyone had finished, he shared the outcome of the trials that he had orchestrated and the amount of money he had made.

There was silence at the table.

Koni asked if Brian was joking.

Brian shared that each of the families involved got around three hundred million dollars, the three lawyers got around thirty-five million each and he came home with about twenty million. He laughed and said that he had orchestrated the trials, but he was paid the least.

Koni asked what he was going to do with so much money.

Brian replied he was thinking of setting up some sort of charity to help less fortunate people. He added that was what he would be thinking about when he walked the beach that afternoon.

Aunt Marian laughed and said that she had always known that he was destined to do great things, but she had never envisioned him making a fortune on his very first legal case.

Kaia laughed and said that from now on she would not worry about taking him up on any vacation invitation that he might offer.

He nodded and said that he was going to separate his finances so that his law-oriented business ventures would be separated from his personal financial ventures. He now owned three homes on Maui and planned to continue to build that up. He also planned to continue his law-oriented business. He added that he might or might not find another such case. He added that his targets were the super-rich that deviated from the norm and had broken the law. He was not sure how long it would take to find the next bad super rich person.

He pointed out that was the work he would do sitting at his desk with a view of Molokini was to search for that next case.

Lunch ended and his father joked that he was ready to carry his suitcase wherever he might need to go.

Brian said that was below his status and that he should think about protecting him as he always had and be his bodyguard instead.

Koni replied that would be too dangerous now.

They parted after a big hug and the exchange of, "I love you."

This happened two more times.

Brian decided to drive right to the beach parking area. He needed badly to not only walk off the huge lunch he had consumed but he planned to use the walk to think through how he was going to handle his finances.

He walked out to the beach on the public entrance that went between the two houses to the beach. As he passed the shower area, he recognized the father of one of his high school friends. He stopped and chatted with him. He found out that his friend was now a sushi chef at one of the top restaurants on Maui and that the family was doing well. He said that he would go to the restaurant and order sushi but only the sushi made by his friend.

He then went out for his walk that went up to Ulua beach.

There were several out cropping of black lava that the waves washed over.  They had pockets or small pools that housed small fish, crabs, and other small sea life in a microcosm world that he always enjoyed examining.  He had come prepared with his water walking shoes so that he would not cut his feet.

He made it up to Ulua beach and turned around.  He was almost back to his starting point when he spotted a very large sand dollar being washed up by the waves.  He knelt down and retrieved it and was carefully washing it off when he realized that two young girls were looking over his shoulders.  He swiveled halfway around and showed them the silver dollar that he had found.

He was explaining the intricacies of the patterns when he felt the presence of someone else looking down.

He looked up and his heart seemed to stop as he looked into the deep green eyes looking down at him.  Her smile melted his madly beating heart.  He had to put a hand down on the sand to keep from falling over.

She commented that it was a beautiful sand dollar and asked what he was planning to do with it.

He said he was planning to give it to the two girls and asked them their names.

He said that he liked the names, Linda and Luarie, and said that the sand dollar that he was giving them was special because it was twice as large as most sand dollars and would be big enough for them to share.

They should make sure to let it dry out before they packed it for its trip home.

He stood up and asked what the name of the mother of such lovely girls might be.

"Annie is what most people call me," was the quiet reply.

He then boldly asked if she would take a walk down the beach with him.

She nodded and said that she needed a moment.

He watched her go over to where a very good-looking Black lady and a tall handsome Black man were sitting on a large black lava rock.

It was clear that the three were all friends.

He was sure that the Black man was at least as tall as he.

Annie returned and as they walked along, she took his hand and asked him his name.

It took him a moment before he could reply.

It was clear to him that he was in the presence of his soul mate. He could not get over the feeling that was running through him.

Annie smiled and said that she too was in a slight state of disbelief. She admitted that she had never looked into someone's eyes and been so shocked. The fact that he had the same green eyes that she saw every morning when she looked into the mirror was the first thing that stunned her.

He stopped at the first pool and showed her the microcosm world that fascinated him.  He commented that at the moment he felt that his macrocosm world had just exploded like a supernova.

He admitted that he was not sure what was going on, but he did not want it to stop.

They continued walking silently holding hands.  When they turned to walk back, Brian knew that no matter what, he would need to get her address.  He was not going to lose the link that he had just made.  He had waited a long time for the feeling that was now going through him.

As they approached the rock where the two Black individuals had been seated, he noted that the tall Black man was sitting and playing tick, tac toe with the two girls.  It was clear to him that both the woman and the man were friends of Annie's.

As they approached Annie introduced the lady as Alex Evercrest and the tall man as Matt Knolton.

Brian shook hands with the two and realized that Matt was at least an inch taller than him.

There was a silent awkward moment but then Alex broke the silence and asked if he could come to a grill out that she was throwing on the following afternoon.

Brian was ecstatic to get such an invite.  He had been wondering how he was going stay connected with Annie.

As he was walking out the father of his high school friend was hosing the sand back to the beach.  He commented that Brian looked like he had seen a ghost.

Brian shook his head and said that it was not a ghost, but he had seen an angel and she had captured his soul.

He crossed the street to the parking lot and drove slowly home. He had no clue who the Black woman was but the fact that she had given him the address of a home he had often admired made him wonder who she was and how rich she might be.

The next morning, he called Malia, one of his high school friends, who had become an investigator on the island police force. She laughed and said that he had met one of the most famous detectives in the country who was known as "Cincinnati's Black Annie Okley."

Her name was Alex Evercrest, and she owned the home that she had invited him to. She added that she and the rest of the department and their significant others would all be at the grill out. She then described the case where Alex had helped the department solve the case of a serial killer a few years back.

Brian commented that he remembered the case but that her name had never surfaced in the news.

He shared that he had met a friend of hers that he was crazy about and hoped to get closer too.

Malia said that if that friend had two beautiful daughters, then she had met that friend. Alex had rescued her and her daughters from the woods in Pennsylvania where she had been chained in captivity for fifteen years and had the two daughters by the kidnapper that had met his end when he tried to shoot Alex.

Malia added that Annie was a very talented artist that had made a fortune from the paintings she had painted during her captivity.

Brian shook his head and said that the situation was getting very complicated, but he knew what he wanted. He thanked Malia for the information and said that he would get the rest from Annie.

He spent the rest of the day Googling the internet as he dug into both Annie's and Alex's background.

He took the time to look at the paintings that Annie had for sale and picked one that featured a view of the ocean and a piece of Molokini seen through the lens of a crack in black stone. He found out that the painting was currently only available on Maui at the address to which he had been invited.

He immediately bought and paid for it. He was surprised at the price, but he was keen on buying it. He was able to add a note with the payment saying that he would personally pick it up.

The cases that had been solved by Alex were numerous and seemed to span the country east, west, north, and south. It even touched Europe. He was fascinated by the number and breadth of her cases and figured it would take him a lot longer to really understand her capabilities. He figured that would be an effort worth his time and that he would learn a ton by doing his homework on her.

He decided that with so many people driving to that home far out along a very narrow road, parking would be at a premium. He figured his moped would be the better transport to use for the grill out.

The day cooperated by being a clear cloudless day.  He had worn his swim trunks as instructed and when he arrived it was just as he suspected, parking was at a premium, but he was able to put his moped between a red Mercedes parked by the gate and the stone wall.

He walked in through the small gate and walked to the front door.  He was caught up by the fascinating appearance of the door that had embedded shells and other sea life encapsulated in clear plastic that were backlit.  He stood admiring it before ringing the doorbell.

The person that greeted him was a service employee that he knew from high school.  She had been a year or two ahead of him.  He greeted her and let her know that he had been two years behind her in the same high school.  She guided him out to the back to where the barbeque was just starting.

Alex greeted him and said that Annie had shared the fact that he had bought the painting that she had just finished and was barely dry.  She took his hand and guided him to a spot and pointed out where he could see a piece or Molokini.  He stood there fascinated by the view.  It was the view on the painting.

He looked at Alex and commented that the view was magnificent and almost as beautiful as her friend.

He turned to find that Annie was standing behind him smiling.

It did not matter.  He was so happy to see her again.

She gave him a hug and asked if he wanted to go for a quick swim.  She took his hand and guided him along toward the opening at the end.  She then pulled him around the end of the opening and wrapped her arms around him and gave him a passionate kiss.

A shiver ran through him as he responded.  After a few moments, Annie asked him where he had come up with the money to buy a painting that she had priced to keep it from selling.

He joked that he had gone to the biggest bank in Maui and robbed it so that he could buy it.

She said that she would need to hold it for a few more days to make sure the paint dried, and the painting was saleable.

She took his hand and said that she needed to get back to the grill out before she went too far with him.

He nodded and said that he agreed and that he would see about having her stay a few extra days on Maui until the paint on the painting dried.

Once they were back amongst the crowd, Annie pointed to the back corner of the yard where there were two chairs below a low hanging palm tree.  She grabbed an iced tea and handed one to him.

They sat down and she asked him to describe his life on Maui.

Brian said that he had a very good life.  His mother was a prostitute that had moved to Maui from Oregon because of the weather.  She had met and gotten pregnant by an Irish playboy that she had fallen in love with but to whom she was just a vacation fling.

She, when diagnosed with a fatal disease for which there was no cure, had contacted that Irishman and let him know that he was the father of a five-year-old boy.  His biological father had responded by setting up a trust fund seeded with sixty thousand dollars in back child support, and which would add one thousand dollars a month until he was eighteen.  His mother had put that trust into the hands of a financial company that had professional money managers.  It grew substantially over the years and so far, had gone untouched.

She had then found him the home where he ended up growing up with two people that he now considered his parents.

He had gone to University in Ireland because he wanted to seek out his father and because the University gave him a full scholarship and a stipend.

This let him go to college without touching the nest egg that had been turned over to him when he turned eighteen.  He had seen his biological father, his wife and his three half siblings but he had not contacted them.

He had then gone on and earned his master's degree at Stanford and afterwards had gotten a law degree and then obtained his law license in both California and Hawaii.

He ended by saying he was not into practicing law in front of a judge but in the practice of putting billionaire cheats in front of the judge and that he had just finished putting one such billionaire in prison for the rest of his life.

Annie nodded and said that it sounded like a good life and that even though it had a sad beginning it had been all uphill with what seemed to be rich and rewarding results.

She then began her story and how on the day that she had turned thirteen and was on the way to her friend's house to show her the new dress that her mother had bought her, and a neighbor had kidnapped her and taken her to a remote cabin deep in the forest of Pennsylvania where she ended up being chained for fifteen years.  Her kidnapper did not mistreat her other than keeping her chained.  He wanted her to love him but there was no way that was ever to be.  He provided her with books and art supplies.  When she came of age, he had sex with her every other weekend when he came up from Cincinnati to stay at the cabin. Linda and Laurie were the result of his visits and actions.

She had worked at getting herself free and finally one day she had been able to get the cement post that her chain was attached to dug up and she was able to get that post on a wagon that she pulled as she tried to get away.

She spent a week pulling the wagon with the cement post as she tried to get out of the forest and to civilization.

She admitted that her efforts were a total failure.  She had traveled in a large circle and was almost back to the point where she had started when a Black woman came running across the open field and stopped her.  She showed her a picture of her parents and kept repeating that she was a friend.

Annie pointed to Alex and commented that it was the first time she had met her.  She added that now she considered her more than just a friend.

The person who had kidnapped her was about to shoot her, when Alex had stood in front of her and took the shot in her chest.  As the bullet drove her back, Alex had been able to fire two shots that killed him.  Even in that wounded state Alex had grabbed both Linda and Laurie and carried them away from the scene.

That time in the woods was a very long period that was a very long low period life and everything else has been uphill and very fulfilling.

She then added that she had been married shortly to a very nice young man who had been her schoolgirl heart throb.  He was a kind, gentle soul, but he ended up with a brain tumor that once discovered, took him almost immediately.

I had hundreds of paintings that Alex helped get on the market that turned me into a millionaire.  I have a very successful painting career and my two girls are picking up some of that skill, but they are into enjoying school, being active in sports and having parties with their friends.

Matt is their favorite "Uncle" who has played with them from the first time they met him.  Alex is their "Aunt" who they treasure and who inspires them.  Alex's detective partner, Trey has a son Nolan who is now their best friend and who the two currently argue about who gets to marry him.

As for me, I have two loving parents who are just getting ready to retire who have provided me with the support I needed to recover from fifteen years of being chained in the woods.

Brian was silent for a moment, then he commented that he was thinking about the best way to continue to understand each other.  He added that he could only think of one way to do that and that was to spend more time together and continue talking through their feelings.

He then asked when she was going back to Cincinnati.

Annie replied that they were all going back on the Saturday flight.

Brian asked if she might be able to stay until her painting was dry.

54

## **<u>Chapter 6: Next Steps</u>**

Annie had never experienced the feelings going through her mind, heart, and soul.  Later, as she sat slowly sipping on her cup of tea talking with Alex, she shared the fact that she wanted to stay another week in Maui to see if what she had felt in the last two days was a feeling that would continue.  She asked if Alex would consider taking Linda and Laurie home to their grandparents.

Alex smiled and said that she had no problem taking the girls. She added that she hoped that the feeling would continue since she had a good feeling about Brian.  She shared that she had talked with him during the grill out and was impressed with his keen sense of what fairness and justice was all about.  He felt to her as a kindred spirit in his approach to getting the bad guy in front of a judge and letting the law and his peer group decide guilt and met out the punishment.  She pointed out that he had a laser focus on the top financial cheats.  She added that she had one in Cincinnati that she had suggested to him.

Annie thanked Alex and said that she would then plan to stay and see if what she had experienced in the last two days was real. She added that she hoped so.

Brian had a similar conversation with Kaia, who listened and knew at once that Annie had made a life altering impact on him. She shared the fact that her romance with her Koni had been one that had built up over the years they had known each other.  It was a slow romance and one that had so far continued to grow and flourish.  She admitted that she did not know what advice to give to him.

She reminded him that he had so far been the architect of the journey that he was pursuing and that so far, he had been hitting homeruns.  She suggested that he think through the next steps of his romance and then let his intellect guide him as it had guided him so far.  She reminded him of the guiding principle of treating others the way you wish to be treated.  She then said that in this case he should treat romance as a treasure that should be embraced but should be examined as if it was its own entity.

The conversation helped Brian immensely.  He decided that he needed to guide his passion so that it was not the sexual part of the attraction that drove it.  He decided that it needed to be the mental part that was the part that needed to be allowed to flourish and grow.  He needed to make sure that the two of them were equal in how they responded mentally to the world around them.

He was sure of his passion and had the immediate opinion of Annie's mind, but he would focus on how compatible their minds were.

He was not looking for agreement from her. He was looking for strength in how she thought and responded to him. Compliance on her part would only weaken the relationship.

He called Annie to find out what her decision about staying was. He was ecstatic to find out that she was planning to stay. He offered his guest bedroom to her with the explanation that he did not want her stay to be an expensive one but an enjoyable one. He said that he would be glad to pick her up whenever she was ready.

Annie suggested that he pick her up at the airport after Alex and the kids left for the mainland.

He decided that a walk-through the Io valley state park, a visit to the church where sister Ela served and then a dinner in one of his favorite restaurants on the northside would be a good start. He checked on his small supply of wine and decided he needed to stock up as well as get the right snacks for the evening. He had to rein in his enthusiasm to keep from over planning everything. This was new to him, and he knew he was sailing in uncharted waters.

He parked his car in the airport short term parking and walked to the departure area. He was in time to see Alex, Matt, and the kids off. He got a surprise hug from both Linda and Laurie who told him to be nice to their mother.

He let them know that was what he had in mind.

Alex smiled and told him that he had made a strong impression on her and that she would guide him to a very rich person in Cincinnati that met his criteria for attention.  She was not sure he met the billionaire bar, but he probably met the cheater bar.

Brian thanked her and said that he would certainly consider the person she had in mind.

Matt shook his hand and wished him good luck with his romance with Annie.

Annie surprised him by giving him a hug and a full kiss.  She laughed as she stepped back and commented that he had turned red in the face.  The two of them stood holding hands until Alex and the rest disappeared as they went through security.

Brian shared what he had planned for the rest of the afternoon.  He took the suitcase that Annie had and pulled it back to the parking lot where he had parked his new maroon Pilot.  He then shared what he had planned.

The two of then wandered the trails of Io Park making small talk and commenting on the charming views that each area provided.  They watched the local children enjoying themselves in the water of the two streams flowing through the park.

Annie pointed to the fun that the kids were having and that it made the park seem vibrant and alive.

Brian felt a calm and easy flow of vibes between them.  He hoped that Annie was having a similar experience.

Annie in fact was having an experience that she thought of as a flower slowly opening its petals to the warming sun.  She let the feeling flow and calm her.  It was a feeling that she had never experienced before.  It was a feeling she hoped would last a lifetime.  It removed any doubt about her decision to stay.

Brian led the way back to the car and said the next stop was at the church where his biological mother had received guidance that had led him to his current life.

After parking, he led the way into the small church.  He hoped that Sister Ela would be there.  He had not seen her for almost ten years and wondered whether she would still be at the church.

He was not disappointed.  Sister Ela came up the aisle and greeted him as if he were a regular.  She commented that she had talked to his Makuahine just a few days prior and had learned about her star lawyer.  She smiled, looked to Annie, and asked why she would have any interest in such a dull, lawyer.

Annie returned the smile and replied it was because he had magic in his kiss.

Sister Ela nodded and said that the magic was not in the kiss but in the soul and that she was sure of the power of his soul.

Brian invited Sister Ela to a grill out at his home in Wailea on the coming Friday.

She replied that she wouldn't miss it.

As they walked out Annie asked when he had decided on a grill out.

Brian chuckled and said that it was while he was talking to Sister Ela.  He went on to say that he hoped to parade his new sweetheart around and show his success at attracting only the most beautiful one.

Annie laughed and said that too much honey on a slice of bread just ran over the edge and was wasted.  But then she gave him a hug and a kiss.

The timing was just right for an early dinner and Brian drove to one of his favorite mom and pop restaurants that featured the best fillet mignon that he had ever eaten.  In the past he had been a regular and as he entered, he was greeted with a hug by Estrella and led to his favorite outside table.  He asked about her son, who had been on the same football team as him.

She put up her hand and returned inside.  A few moments later Eduardo, his old teammate, came out.  He was wearing a chef's hat that declared him the head chef on the Island of Maui.

Eduardo pointed at his head and said that Maui was his world, so he figured he was the best chef in the world.

After the two exchanged a hug, Brian introduced Annie.

Eduardo commented that she must be special if she was out with the person who had been named as the one to be a perpetual bachelor by everyone in their high school class.

Annie gave Eduardo a hug and replied that she had waited until Brian was ready before making her move.

Eduardo asked if they were interested in one or several of his variations of famous beef dishes.

He said that he prepared a Hawaiian version of Bistecca alla Fiorentina that featured a nice, charred crust on the outside of an inch thick steak while the inside remained a succulent red.

He also had a Hawaiian version of Espetada served with the juices of the skewered meat soaked up by a thick slice of crusty garlic bread that he had baked.

He described the third choice as his Hawaiian Alcatra, his version of a Brazilian Churrasco whose thinly pink sliced meat was highlighted with a Hawaiian flavored sweet sauce.

He added that each dish had rice, grilled asparagus and a small side salad that rounded out the meal.

He then said that a drink of their choice was on him.

Brian replied that all of the choices sounded great and that in the next week he would come back so that the two of them could enjoy each of them.  He looked at Annie and asked her what sounded best to her.

Annie chose the Bistecca ala Fiorentina.

Shortly after Eduardo went in, his mother came out and said that they were in for a treat because Eduardo had become the best chef that she had ever raised.

Brian laughed and said that he thought Eduardo was an only child.

She smiled and said that he still was the best chef she had ever raised and asked what drinks she could bring out for them.

Brian asked if she had a Hawaiian Red Cahors.

Estrella said that of course she did and asked Annie what she might want.

Annie replied that she would take the same as Brian.

The dinner was what Annie described as a lunch to die for. She complimented Eduardo on the wonderful flavor of the steak and the nice crisp exterior that was a nice contrast to the soft interior.

After dinner they drove up to the first falls on the road to Hanna and Brian led the way up the path to the base of the falls. He pointed to the split of the water at the top of the falls and said that this was where Alex had cornered and then shot and killed the Maui serial killer a few years ago.  He said that he had learned from one of his friends that was one of the detectives in the case, that it was Alex that had solved it.  This was the first time he had recently stopped at the falls and that it was at the top of the right side of the fall where the serial killer slit the throat of his victim and then jumped down into the pool to swim in the water and their blood.

He then led Annie up the back side trail up to the top of the falls and they both looked at the point where the victim would have been standing.

Annie said that it was creepy and that it brought back memories of her own captivity and the moments of her moments of insanity as she tried hard to remain sane and to keep going. She took Brian's hand and led the way back to the car.  She said she was ready for the next part of the day.

Brian suggested they take a walk along the beach to decompress, and he then apologized for bringing back bad memories.

Annie shook her head and said that she would slowly take him through her experiences but that she would set the pace and that many memories were good ones but set in the backdrop of being a chained prisoner in the woods.

As they walked along the beach, Brian said that dinner was going to be at the place that he called home with the two people that he considered his mother and father.

Annie asked whether it was her approval appearance.

Brian laughed and said that though the two had always been his sounding-boards, they had little to say about who he fell in love with. He stopped and took Annie in his arms and gave her a kiss. Then he took her hand and led the way back to his car.

He said that he had one more stop before driving up to his parents' home. He stopped at a flower shop and bought a bouquet of red roses and a single stem of a yellow rose. He said that the red roses were for the person he considered his mother and the yellow one was for his biological mother that he would introduce her to.

The drive up to the home he had grown up in took about thirty minutes.

He stopped halfway up the small road leading up to the parking area. He got out and walked to the back of the Pilot and pointed out to Molokini, Kaho'olawe and Lanai and said that this was the scene burned permanently in his mind. He had grown up with it and now his home had a closer view of that scene.

He then drove the rest of the way up the long lane. When they arrived, Brian commented that the extra car in the parking area meant that Annie would also get to meet the person he considered his aunt.

He got out and opened the back of the Pilot. He took the single yellow rose and walked to where a now bare rose bush stood at the edge of the yard with the same view that he had stopped a few moments ago to admire. He put the rose into the branches of the rose bush and said that he had planted the rose bush when he had graduated from high school and was ready to leave for Ireland. He added that it was planted over the ashes of his biological mother who had always loved yellow roses.

Annie remained quiet. She knew that Brian was not expecting her to say anything but that he was merely providing context for her to absorb. She knew that she would have many similar moments of sharing that would need no comment.

She took the bottle of white wine that Brian said was for his aunt.

He carried a case of mixed local brew beer, a bottle of champaign and a dozen roses and led the way to the side door that led to the kitchen.

Akaia came over and took the roses and the champaign and put them on the table and then gave Brian a hug.  Brian put down the beer and then introduced Annie.

Akaia went around the table and gave Annie a hug.  She commented that she was the first woman that Brian had ever brought to the house.

She then introduced Lilian Nelson, a longtime family friend.

Brian added that before becoming his aunt Lilian, she was his phycologist who had helped him through some confusing early years and who still shared her wisdom that provided the foundation that he now stood on.

Annie handed Lilian the white wine and added that Brian had made sure that he had a gift of a wine that he knew she loved.

Lilian thanked Brian and added that it had been more than three months since he last had lunch at the house and now, he was bringing a beautiful woman to introduce to them.

She took Annie's hand and suggested they take a walk around the property.  She said that she had plenty of interesting gossip about Brian.

Annie was surprised but went along.  The next thing she found herself doing was sharing her own history.  It was more than an hour later when the call for dinner was made.  On their walk back, Annie saw that a dark green pickup was parked next to Brian's SUV.

Lilian commented that she considered their conversation as private between the two of them.

Annie nodded and thanked her.

She was surprised when they entered the house and was introduced to Koni who came to her and gave her a hug and whispered that she must be special since she was the first to ever have been brought to the house.

## **Chapter 7: Cincinnati**

The week together went much too fast for both of them. Brian hired his chef friend to cater for the pool side grill out with the stipulation that the friend would be a guest and those he hired would attend to the grilling and catering. He also hired a small three-piece band to play casual music. He wanted the atmosphere to be enjoyable but have some ambience. Everyone at the barbecue had interacted with Annie sometime during the week and were well aware that the celebration was to welcome her into the fold of his friends.

The pool side barbeque was in full swing and in the full interrogation mode. Annie was constantly in one conversation or another. The focus seemed to be on her two daughters.

Brian caught on to what the questioning was about. He retrieved a picture that Annie had taken of him and the two girls and gave it to her and told her to proudly show all his friends her two beautiful daughters.

That approach seemed to turn the situation into a positive one and soon that line of questioning moved into one of what was next.  Annie was relieved and warmed by Brian's approach to that situation.  He had interjected himself and let everyone know that what was to happen next was a lifetime of living.

Then she was surprised when Brian announced that he was flying to Cincinnati with her on the following day.  This was a surprise that he had kept secret until his announcement.  She had been dreading leaving and suddenly she was wondering how long he would stay in Cincinnati.

The barbeque ended slowly as his friends left.  Akaia, Koni, and Lilian were the last to leave.  They all wished the two a good trip and said they were eager to see them and the girls back in Maui.

That evening Annie asked why Brian had decided to accompany her.

He smiled and said that she had endured the scrutiny of his friends and he figured he would do the same with her friends.

The trip to Cincinnati was long but uneventful.  They arrived and drove Annie's practical Odessey to a very impressive looking home in an eastern suburb.  After unloading their luggage, Annie called her parents to let them know she was back and would be over to pick up the girls.  She accepted an invitation for dinner after checking with Brian, who gave her a positive nod.

After hanging up she warned him that he would get the, "what are your intentions" question from her father.  She added if he wanted to shock him, he should respond, "to sleep with your daughter every chance I get."

Brian laughed and said that at least he would be telling the truth.

A short time later they arrived at her parents' house and went in.

The greetings were rather formal except for the hug he got from Linda and Laurie.  That seemed to have the effect of changing the atmosphere more into a family affair.

Linda, Annie's mother made the point that she was called Linda and her name's sake was called Lin when they were both in the same room.  Brian said that made sense and it was easy.

He walked around the living room and took in three of Annie's paintings and then Stanley took him and showed him the paintings in the entrance hall, the ones up the stairs and the ones along the upstairs hallway.

Brian joked about the fact that he was not sure he could afford so many of Annie's paintings after having to pay more than three hundred thousand dollars for the one he owned.

Linda looked at Annie and asked how she could possibly charge him that much.

Annie said that she had put what she thought was an outrageous price on that painting to keep it from selling and had been amazed when some unknown person bought it anyway.

She laughed and added that now she was now holding on to the payment to make sure she could keep the buyer as well as to get the painting back.

Brian smiled and said that he already had the painting hung over the mantle in his Maui home so that he could keep it and attract its painter to spend time there.

Linda shook her head and commented that life in the Scott family was going to take on a rather new but interesting turn. She then shared the fact that they were all invited to a grill out at Alex's work partner's house the following afternoon.

Annie smiled and looked at Brian and said that it would be his turn to run the questioning gauntlet.

Brian nodded and said that he would go armed with the same picture he had given her, but he would make the point that three beautiful women were his reason for a lifelong love affair.

The next afternoon, Lindsey and her son Nolan greeted them at the door.  She welcomed Annie's parents and led them out toward the backyard.

Nolan and the two girls went off on their own.

Alex and Matt were out talking to a tall broad-shouldered individual that Lesley said was her husband, Trey.

Annie took Brian by the hand and went out to the grill.

Brian shook hands with Trey, got a hug from Alex and another from Matt.  After getting caught up with Matt and Alex he turned to find that eight more people were coming into the backyard.

This time Alex took his hand and guided him over and introduced the arriving guests.  She first introduced, the "Chief," and his wife, then Bill and his wife, Trevor. and his wife and finally she pointed to Johnnie who she said was her "Wizard," and the beautiful lady was Mary.

She then pointed to him and announced that she had met a kindred soul whose goal was to put the bad guy in front of a judge and a jury of his peers.

The Chief smiled and said that having one kindred soul working for him was all he could handle so there would be no job offer coming from him.

Brian smiled and replied that luckily, he was not looking for a job but was here to see about a bad guy that Alex had in mind.

Trey had come over and asked who that bad guy might be.

Alex looked up at him and asked him to guess who she would most like to have in Brian's cross hair.

Trey smiled and said there was only one that he could think of was and he carried the pretentious name of Samuel Herington III.

The Chief shook his head and said he did not want to know anything about it and walked over to the grill to get himself a brat.

Johnnie asked whether Brian had a research analyst that he used.

Brian said that he did not.

Johnnie asked if he knew Leilani Dickens, the chief of Detectives in Maui.

Annie laughed and said that Leilani had just grilled her about her intentions towards Brian at the celebration cookout that he had hosted before they had left Maui.

Johnnie said that she had linked him up with Kekoa Dalavan a native Hawaiian who he had worked with on the Pool of Blood case. He added that he was currently living on Oahu but was originally from the Big Island. He added that the two of them had worked together and he had shared all his hacking techniques with him. He suggested that Kekoa might be interested in an opportunity to work for Brian.

Brian thanked him and said he would put in a call to Leilani to see if she would check out Kekoa's interest in being an analyst and online investigator for him.

Brian looked to see what time it was in Hawaii and decided to make a call to Leilani and stepped away from the group.

The conversation of the grill out seemed to focus on Brian's experience, his interest in seeking out cheating billionaires and his life in Hawaii. It was clear to Annie that her friends accepted Brian.

She also realized that they only knew about her and were very familiar with her life after her escape from captivity in the woods. She had no middle school or high school friends because she had grown up chained in the woods. She knew that her time there would affect her and be with her for the rest of her life.

She was so grateful to have made the friends that she had since her escape and now to have found the person who seemed to embrace her both in body and soul. The fact that she was now a successful artist and had two wonderful girls and had a gorgeous home all were factors that provided her with balance and stability.

She sat and enjoyed listening to Alex share her opinion of Samuel Herington III. It was clear that Alex had no respect for him or the way he practiced law. Alex pointed out that Samuel had many shady contacts who were on the wrong side of the law and had recently tried to swindle money from a man who had lost his wife.

Johnnie had an even greater contempt for the man.

She could not help but laugh when Johnnie said that he was always surprised how soiled the toilet paper became when he wiped his Herrington.

Brian was sensitive to the fact that he was not getting questioned about his relationship with Annie. He decided to move the focus from what he was doing by asking who owned a signed Annie Scott painting. When every person raised their hand, he laughed and said that now he knew that they all made too much money because she had charged him more than three hundred thousand for just one.

They all looked at Annie and ask how she could do such a thing.

She pointed to Brian and said that was going to cost him.  The next painting was going to be sold to him at twice the price.  But she really wanted to go give him a hug for changing the focus of the conversation.

The rest of the talk was about what each of them was going to do.  She said that she was going to do a series of paintings about her recent stay in Hawaii and then she was going to put on an exhibit featuring her paintings along with a group of past and current Hawaiian artists.

Brian got an invitation to lunch at the riverfront from Alex.  She said she would share more detailed information about Samuel Herrington III.  She added that after that she would step away from the case because she did not want to muddy the legal issues.

He thanked her and let her know that he would decide about pursuing the case after getting a good look into the situation and his ability to get the data he needed.

Johnnie volunteered to help him during his off hours until he could hire his own online sleuth.  He added that he had a deep desire to make sure that Brian took the case.

Brian thanked him and said that he had asked Leilani about Kekoa, and she had replied that he had mentioned the desire for a more challenging job, but that he was not willing to move away from Hawaii, so he figured he was stuck.  He had asked Leilani to make Kekoa an offer to come work for him.

Brian had mentioned the salary figure he had in mind and laughed when Leilani said she was willing to learn to hack for that kind of salary.  Brian let her know that he was interested in interviewing Kekoa in the next few days because he needed his help almost immediately.

He met Alex for lunch the next day at River Front Park.  He knew that he was sitting on the lawn looking at the spot where Alex had opened her first case.  He was surprised how peaceful and serene the park felt.  He could see a coal barge being pushed by a tug as it went slowly by.

The brown water of the river disappointed him in the sense that it did not feel pollution free but felt polluted to him.

Johnnie had carried out a large pizza and Matt had carried out the drinks and a bag of French fries and onion rings.

Alex asked what Annie was up to.

Brian said that she had gone to her art shop and was painting and working with her partner on setting up the art show that she had in mind.

He added that she had said to let Alex know that she wanted to have lunch with her and Matt on the coming weekend.  She had suggested a bike ride along the Loveland bike path and that Linda and Laurie would also be along for the ride.

Trey spoke up and said that Lesley had let him know about the invitation and that Nolan had already said that he wanted to go.  So, it seemed that they would have a good crowd bicycling.

Brian said that he had a great bike back at his house in Maui and asked where he could get one in the Cincinnati area.

Alex recommended the bicycle shop she frequented and said she would give them a call and arrange for them to show him any model he might be interested in.

Johnnie asked whether he could join the outing.

Alex laughed and said he could join if he made her and Matt breakfast before going on the ride.

Johnny joked back that breakfast would require a batch of her oatmeal cookies to make sure it was properly prepared.

Brian asked if this was a normal exchange or was, he a witness to bribery and counter bribery going on.

Trey nodded and said that he was observing the normal exchange that constantly went on between the two.

Brian's phone rang and after answering he walked down to the walk where the body of Alex's first case had been and stood and listened to Leilani as she described her conversation with Kekoa and the fact that he was super excited about the opportunity. She said that she had not shared the salary that Brian had mentioned and would leave that up to him. She gave him Kekoa's phone number and said that he was anxious to hear from him.

Brian hung up and called Kekoa. He introduced himself and asked whether Kekoa was interested in working for him. He added that he could stay on Oahu or live on any island that was more comfortable for him. Working from home was acceptable but it would be great to have a couple of days together each week at the beginning of their working relationship. He then gave him the starting salary.

Kekoa asked if he had heard the offer correctly.

When Brian repeated the offer, Kekoa let out a whoop and said that he wanted to live next door to his new boss.

Brian laughed and said that would probably be possible because he had seen several homes for sale in his Maui neighborhood.

Brian let Kekoa know that he would probably get a call from Johnnie Smith who had volunteered to share his improved legal analysis programs, as well as his other tools.

Kekoa said that he would gladly take in Johnnie's improved tools. He shared that Johnnie was one of the best hacks that he had ever been privileged to learn from.

Brian said that he would plan to meet with Kekoa in the coming week and suggested they agree on several calls in the coming days. He then asked Kekoa to see what he could learn about a Samuel Harrington the III. He wanted background information, people he had communicated with or had represented and the courts that he had used. He wanted to know about his high school, college years, and law experience.

Kekoa commented that he really needed to talk with Johnnie.

Brian walked back to where Johnnie was now sitting by himself and learned that Alex had returned to her office.

He asked what Johnnie was planning for the rest of the afternoon and learned that he was planning to work from his apartment.

He asked if it was possible for him to give his new analyst a call and help him get started in his new role.

## **<u>Chapter 8: The Johnnie of Hawaii</u>**

Kekoa picked up the phone and heard a voice that he had not heard for some time.  He was surprised by what she shared with him.  He had just spent the day thinking about his career and more or less had shrugged his shoulders in resignation that he would just have to continue doing what he had been doing.  He wanted a different job, but he did not want to leave the islands. He traveled home to the big island often to see friends and his parents and visited the other islands to enjoy hiking, surfing and just lazing.  It was the life he wanted and there had been no jobs that he sought available.  He had no desire to move to the continent.

Now, the Chief of Detectives on Maui, Leilani, was talking to him about the job of being an analyst and computer specialist for a young lawyer who had just made a small fortune putting a less than honest billionaire into jail.  She had likened the role being offered to that of Johnnie Smith who he had worked with a few years back to get the evidence on a serial killer on Maui.

He gave a small laugh when she made the comparison and said he was just a shadow of what Johnnie was somehow able to do.  She said if he were interested, she would pass his phone number on to Brian O'Neill who ran his business out of a home on Maui.  He should expect a call from him.

He hung up and began filling out his resignation paperwork for his current job.  He knew his answer before any call.  He was so eager that the time seemed to crawl.  He hoped the call would come in before it was time to go home.

That did not happen.  The call came in as he sat down at the kitchen table for a snack before going to the beach for a walk.

As soon as he knew it was the call from Brian, he felt like saying yes, he was eager to be his online sleuth, but kept quiet and listened.

Brian explained what he was after and asked if he was interested.

Kekoa finally got to say the yes, he had been waiting to say.  He had not even thought about what the salary might be and when Brian shared the salary he had in mind and asked if it met his expectations he almost fell out of his chair.  He stood up and wanted to shout but he refrained from doing so.  He politely answered that it was more than what he had expected, and it was exceedingly generous.

He knew immediately that he was going to enjoy working for Brian when he heard him say that he could lower the offer to a level where it would just being OK.  He laughed and said that the offer was generous, and he was very happy about it and eager to show that he was worth it.

After agreeing to meet with Brian face to face in the coming week and being told that Johnnie would be calling to get him up to speed on the latest investigative techniques, he again thanked Brian for considering him.  Brian replied that he should thank Johnnie because he was the one who had recommended him.

Kekoa hung up and danced around the room as he realized that not only had he been offered a job that almost doubled his salary, but he was going to be able to stay on the Islands and he was going to do something that would be super challenging.

He went for his beach walk, singing the states anthem, "Hawai'i Pono'ī" ("Hawaii's Own").

The timing of Johnnie's call seemed to be timed with his return from his walk.  He was still humming the tune of Hawaii's state song and had trouble getting the tune out of his mind.

He flipped open the computer and went online to meet with Johnnie.

What Johnnie shared blew his mind and greatly impressed him with the improved automated hacking capabilities that he had developed.  It seemed to him that Johnnie had automated most of the approaches to getting through the firewalls that most organizations had.

He asked Johnnie if he had been using AI to help him. Johnnie had replied that doing so would have kept him in the same game that everyone else was in, and he used his own hacking logic and made sure it was backward and upside down just like his mind.

Kekoa knew he was talking to some sort of computer savant because he knew that Johnnie had only been in his current role for a few years and had started to do his hacking close to the age of seventy.

He called Leilani the next morning and asked where Brian lived.  He then looked for homes that might be on sale nearby. He found one that was about a five-minute drive away in a gated community that had a great view of the water and the road that went to Lahaina and the windmills on the ridge.  He toured it via the internet and knew it was what he had often dreamt of having. It was expensive enough that he had second thoughts but decided that he was going to try it.  He noted that it had been on the market for more than six months.  He put in his bid and hoped it would be enough.

He then went through a series of financial calculations and figured that he was at his limit, but he would be able to handle the purchase.  By selling his condo on Oahu he would have the money for a down payment.

# Hawaiian Phoenix

He put the idea of buying a new car out of his mind. His old car would have to do for the next few years. His current laptop computer and two screen set up would also have to do. He figured he would have to cook most of the time. It was definitely a stretch, but timing was everything.

He had been working with a realtor about selling his condo and she had let him know that she had two interested clients. He figured if he won the bid for the house on Maui, he would release his condo for sale.

He put that behind him and decided to focus on learning the new hacking techniques that Johnnie had sent him. He decided to hack into his own bank account to see if he could do so undetected. He laughed when he realized that he could instantly increase his wealth with a couple of finger strokes if he wanted to risk being the one that Brian sent to jail.

He decided that he would focus on getting the information on Samuel Herrington III, the name that Johnnie had given him. He got into that bank account as easily as he had his own. He looked over the records and found the routing numbers of other bank accounts to which money had been transferred to and from. He organized his search and began documenting each bank separately. There were two banks in the US, in Miami and Tampa and three offshore, one in St. Lucia, one in Jamaica, and one in Puerto Rico. He went into each and noted the amounts that were being held. He discovered that each of the banks was investing this money into a portfolio of stocks.

He tabulated the total amount of money that was being managed and came up with that it was close to three billion dollars.

He wondered how a practicing lawyer could legally make that much money.

He then looked up what Samuel paid in taxes and found out that he was only claiming an income of three hundred fifty thousand dollars with one hundred fifty thousand dollars of expenses. He paid almost nothing in taxes but was making more than one hundred ninety million dollars a year!

He wondered about the source of the three billion dollars and went back in bank records to examine cash flow over the years and to see if he could determine where the money had originated.

He was surprised to find himself still working at five in the morning and decided to get some sleep. He knew that he was now hooked on his new job and that with the tools he had received from Johnnie, he was going to be able to make a huge contribution. He now had a goal of having a detailed report to share with Brian when they met later in the week.

He sent a message to Brian that they should meet on Maui and that he planned to have a surprise for him.

Brian received his message and wondered what his new employee was up to. He wondered what the surprise might be. He did not know what Kekoa and Johnnie had done in the last couple of days because he had concentrated on nurturing his new relationship with Annie.

She had a great arrangement in Cincinnati and had the two girls in a very good school. He had researched Maui and had contacted the nearest public high school and talked with the principal and the director of grade curriculum. They had invited him to come in and visit them. He figured that would be appropriate if Annie was with him.

There was a second option also near where he lived that was more innovative in that they had both in classroom sessions but also offered what they called distance learning.

He was not sure which school would best fit the girls. He knew that first he would need to test the waters of having them move to Hawaii. He was somewhat hesitant to do so immediately but he was going to discuss it with Annie to get her reaction.

Annie had also been dealing with the issue of where she should live. She had great friends in Cincinnati as did the two girls. She was torn about the situation because she also knew how much Brian was family-oriented and that meant he wanted to live in Hawaii. Both she and the girls had talked about where to live, and they had indicated that they had some good friends in Cincinnati, but they loved the weather and the beaches of Hawaii. They said that if they were going to move it should be as soon as possible so they could begin to make friends in Hawaii, but they wanted to come back to Cincinnati as often as possible.

When she approached Brian about where they should think of living, she could tell immediately that he had been thinking about the same issue. She suggested they each take turns sharing their thinking before any decision was made.

They gave each other a hug when they realized that they had each done critical research but had each waited to learn what the other was thinking before taking a position on location.

The two did a thorough look into the school options in Hawaii and agreed that the girls would probably be better off in the Technology School that offered distance learning in combination within classroom learning. Educational flexibility would most likely prove to be an advantage.

Annie said she would float the idea with the girls first before bringing him into the loop. She wanted to give them the opportunity to voice their position in an environment that they knew was open and safe.

Brian left the next day for the trip to Hawaii knowing that by the time he landed there he would know how to think about life in the near future.

When he got off the plane in Maui, he was surprised to be met by Kekoa who was holding a three strand Tuberose Lei. Kekoa made the point that the three strands were for the beautiful ladies he had left in Cincinnati. He knew immediately that he and Kekoa were going to get along very well.

It was late afternoon and near dinner time.  He was not exceptionally hungry, but he asked Kekoa whether he was up for dinner and suggested a place near his house.

Kekoa had learned about Brian's love affair from Leilani and had decided that he would meet his new boss at the airport. Leilani had given him a picture of Brian so that he could greet him and had been the one to suggest the three strand Lei.  Brian's reaction to being greeted had sealed the fact that he owed Leilani a big favor for having given him the idea about the Lei.

He had not yet heard back about his offer on the house he wanted but was expecting it over the weekend.  He was currently staying at a bed and breakfast just a few blocks from where he hoped his new home would be.  He was driving a rental car and after getting the luggage he drove back to Wailea to Brian's home.

Brian was surprised to be handed a binder that detailed all the money transactions that Samuel Herrington III had done for most of his professional career.  He was also surprised that Samuel qualified to be one of his billionaire crooks.  The connections with the criminal side of the money flow were going to be very helpful.  As he went through the binder, he asked how many hours Kekoa had spent getting all the information.

Kekoa laughed and said that he needed to catch up on his sleep and there was more information available, but he had run out of time.

Brian asked if Kekoa had by any chance figured out how to get Samuel in front of a judge.  He watched as Kekoa shook his head and replied that clearly the money was coming in from the dark side but unless they could get some direct connection to some sort of bribery or illegal money transfer from a criminal's bank account the amount of money by itself did not make it a crime.  The one point that might be a crime was the amount of money that Samuel paid in taxes.  Tax evasion was the area that would most likely put him behind bars.

Brian said that he agreed and that he would most likely pursue that avenue.  He said that he wanted to do enough digging to make sure they had uncovered all the likely ways to give the prosecution the material that would stand up in court and would allow them to win the case.

He decided to focus the dinner on how the two of them would work together in the coming weeks.

## **Chapter 9: Samuel Herrington III**

Samuel knew he was handsome and that he attracted women like a magnet.  He had a full-length mirror on the wall to the side of his office desk.  He was constantly checking out his appearance and was pleased with what he saw.

"When you are the best, you have to look the best," he thought to himself as he took in his new Stefano Breyer shoes.

This was a new pair, and it was the first day he had worn them.

He knew why he had hired Linda as his secretary when she complemented him on how good his new shoes looked.  He liked the fact that she paid attention to such details.

Samuel needed to decide to what social function to wear his new Testoni suit that he had bought when he had purchased his shoes.  He really wanted to show it off.

A quick motion of his hand put the imagined out of place hair where it belonged, and Samuel turned from the mirror and walked to the door.

He was on the way to a court session.

Linda was old enough to be his mother or maybe even his grandmother.  Early on he had learned that having a young secretary was a problem.  They could be young and ugly and still be a problem.  Linda was great and she knew how to stay on his good side.

Linda looked at Samuel as he walked out the door.  He was by far the most egotistical person she knew and a person who she disliked intensely.  But he was paying her a top dollar salary and he let her do her own office management.

She knew how to manipulate her boss even as he thought of himself as superior to her.  A few compliments on his shoes and clothes went a long way to keep him at bay.

Samuel looked at his reflection in the elevator mirrors on the door.  He thought he cut a fine figure in his Desmond Merrion Supreme suit.  The suit had set him back about the same amount that Linda had paid for her new Toyota.

"But I'm worth it," he thought and smiled to himself as he got on the elevator.  He made sure to only touch the button to the first floor.

He thought about the case he had in front of the judge and shook his head.  His client did not have a snowball's chance of winning, but he had not told him that.  He had taken the case because it was going to be easy, and it was going to be profitable for him.  Making money, not necessarily winning, was always more important than what happened to his client.

He by far won most of his cases but he was very sensitive to who the judge was and whether there was a way to put a hand on the balance of justice.  He found that often if his hand had enough money in it the balance would tilt his way.

He was selective in which court he had his clients have their trial.  He used a variety of courtrooms where he knew that certain gifts helped his clients get the better outcomes.  Many of his clients had deep pockets and over the years he had been able to accumulate a tremendous amount of money.

He had put most of his money into accounts that were offshore.  Those accounts were managed by professional money managers and the money was invested in high growth stocks.  He had arranged it so that they were accounts that had names other than his own so they would not show up on his financial statements.

It appeared on record that he was a successful lawyer that was generous with his pay and had high overhead expenses.  He was well to do but paid a minimum of taxes.  He spent time making sure his accountants had the appropriate documentation to make his tax filing appear to be totally legitimate.

The shadier money that came into his possession from his court representation of figures that were doing business on the wrong side of the law never made the books but was sent by them to the offshore banks.  He constantly rotated which bank was used.

Over the years the money managers had almost doubled the money that he had put away.

He was sure that he had set up a foolproof approach to doing business in both the legal and the more questionable side of the law.

Samuel would not have been so sure of himself had he been able to sit in and listen to the dinner conversation that was happening over four thousand miles away in Hawaii, where he was the center of the conversation.

Brian and Kekoa were celebrating Kekoa's having been able to purchase what he considered the home of his dreams.  It was just up the hill from Brian's golf course fairway view home and had a view of Lanai across the water and the electrical power windmills on the Kealaloloa Ridge.

The talk turned to the report of Samuel's finances and various bank accounts that Kekoa had prepared for Brian.  It was clear to both of them that Samuel had hidden a tremendous amount of money in offshore accounts and had used fictitious names to do so.  They figured that to do so Samuel would also have a set of fake passports.

Brian complemented Kekoa on his hacking skills.  They both knew that the material could not be used in court.  So, they were talking about how a trial that accused Samuel of tax evasion could be handled.

Somewhere the fake IDs had to be documented so that they could be used to obtain the appropriate identification to open the bank accounts.  The trick was going to be finding where that might be.

Brian pointed out that they would need to have the fake identification linked to Samuel and the only way to do so would be to get the person handling the account at each bank to identify Samuel as the person who had the fake name.

Brian suggested that they find out which offshore account was set up first and then look in that area for a likely supplier of fake identification.

Kekoa suggested that one of the early court cases that had a shady character might have been the source of the fake IDs.

It was decided that both ideas warranted looking into.

They decided that Brian would focus on getting the case ready to take to court and Kekoa would search to see if he could find the source of the fake IDs.  He would also identify the person at each bank that had met Samuel in person.

Brian would be the one that went to each bank to meet the person handling the accounts to link Samuel with the person holding the account.

On his return to Cincinnati, he took a side trip to the Caribbean to visit each bank.  Then on getting to Cincinnati decided to find a lawyer that would charge Samuel with tax evasion.

When he arrived, he was surprised when he was met at the airport by Annie.  He saw her as he went up the escalator to the luggage claim area.  He felt like he was rising to meet the morning sunshine.  He got a hug and kiss from her and then they walked hand in hand to the luggage reclaim belt that had suitcases literally piling on top of each other.  He found his suitcase and followed her to the car.

She shared the fact that she had made great progress in setting up the art exhibit that she was planning to do.  She had also finished another painting with a Maui scene she had captured on camera.  She asked how his week in Maui and his return trip had gone and if he had made any progress on his case.

Brian shared the fact that Kekoa was going to be a great addition to his efforts in tracking down the information on the persons that might be of interest in his endeavor.  He shared the fact that Kekoa had already moved to Maui so they could work together there when he was on Maui.

Annie shared the fact that Linda and Laurie both said that they were open to living on Maui.  They did want to be able to return to Cincinnati often so they could keep up with the friends they had.

Brian said he was glad that they were so flexible, and that visiting Cincinnati would be no problem.  He looked at Annie and asked about her flexibility.

Annie said that she could easily set up her stand at pool side and suffer the view from their home with a view of Molokini and Lanai while she enjoyed the sun and cooling breeze.  She added that like the girls she wanted to return often to Cincinnati to keep up with the friends that she had.

On Monday, Brian called Alex and asked if she had a lawyer, she would recommend handling a tax evasion case that he was preparing against Samuel.

Alex said she was surprised at the speed at which he was moving.  She said that her recommendation was John Williams and his partner Hanna Waverly.  They were lawyers that were her friends.  They had handled several cases where Samuel was the defendant's lawyer.

Brian thanked her and then called to set up a meeting with the two.

John asked what his interest was in Samuel.

Brian shared the fact that he had gone into the field of sending cheating billionaires to jail.

John laughed and asked why he was pursuing Samuel.  He added that he did not think he was a billionaire.

Brian said it was a look he had taken as a favor to Alex but as he got into the investigation, he found out that Samuel had amassed several billion dollars in several offshore banks under false names and he had paid no taxes on that money.

Hanna, who had been sitting quietly asked how he wanted to file the case against Samuel.

Brian asked if charging him with tax evasion was a good way.

"It would if you have the proof of failure to pay or a deliberate underpayment of taxes and if you can link him to the offshore accounts," John replied.

Brian nodded and said that he was currently working on finding out where the documents for the fake names were produced so he could get the records to be used in court.

He added that he had his own Johnnie doing the looking which meant that much of what he had learned so far was not admissible in court.

He had the names of the people in each bank that could identify Samuel by site as the person using the various pseudonyms.  They could be brought in as witnesses to link Samuel to the accounts.

He added that he had to find the legal way to inform the IRS how Samuel was funneling money that he was receiving from various underworld clients to the offshore accounts.

John nodded and said that it was the government that was the injured party so Brian would want to enlist someone from the IRS.

He added that once they were shown bank records and understood the magnitude of the money, they would be very interested.  They would seek the maximum penalty that tax evasion allowed and might make the money in each bank a separate case so that they could impose the maximum penalty of five years and two hundred fifty thousand dollars multiple times.

John went on to add that Brian stood to make on average between fifteen to thirty percent of the taxes collected.

Brian asked what John's participation would be and learned that once an IRS lawyer got named, he would most likely sit in the gallery and enjoy watching Samuel squirm. The only way he would be directly involved was if the IRS asked for him to be part of their team.

John went on to say that convicting someone of money laundering meant the prosecution had to show that Samuel knowingly engaged in a financial transaction that was designed to conceal the origins of illegally obtained funds. This would be difficult to do, as the prosecution had to show that Samuel had the intent to defraud. If they believed he had, they would then seek comprehensive background checks, asset tracing, and meticulous internet investigations. They would seek to track down how Samuel was conducting his money transfers.

Brian commented that Kekoa had figured out Samuel's money round tripping designed to make the money being transferred into the final account seem legitimate. By passing money through several transfers the end bank accepted it as a legitimate influx to their account.

Kekoa had also identified smurfing or structuring large sums of money into smaller chunks to avoid the transactions appearing suspicious. By having banks in several countries, Samuel was able to deposit smaller amounts into an account and then have that money transferred to another one of his own accounts.

Samuel also employed the use of shell companies that only existed on paper and had no real operations or assets.  He would pass the money through a series of his shell company transactions to disguise its origin.  Money was sent through several shell companies as "payments" for fictitious goods and low risk services.  These shell companies were all registered in the Caribbean in countries with lax money transaction regulations and privacy laws making it easier and better for him to hide his activities.  His various ways to move money took advantage of the complexity of international laws and regulations.  He manipulated invoices or the value of goods in order to move money around and give it the appearance of being legitimate.  Moving funds through different countries, with the involvement of several of his businesses, made it easier for him to evade the standard Anti-Money Laundering (AML) scrutiny checks.  He knew that traditional AML checking approaches looked for patterns in relational databases of the stored data so he made sure that his actions would be random.  He had worked meticulously to ensure that there was not any money laundering red flags in his cash flow.

He never moved large amounts of cash.  He used the countries with weak laws and stayed away from transferring money back to the US from them.

His shell companies were all registered to produce low risk services and products even though none of them were more that entities on paper.

Once he set up an account, he did not change the information associated with them.  He had visited each bank to set up the account under his pseudonym and then had done all the remaining transactions via his shell companies.

Kekoa had used low level financial signals within various data bases as the key to detecting Samuel's money laundering schemes.  The investigation routines he used were ones that he had learned from Johnnie and modified to fit the financial industry that he was scrutinizing.  His routines were able to identify and detect the money laundering signals, and made for a swift, precise, and intuitive way to analyze Samuel's data.

Hanna said she was amazed that Brian had amassed all that information in such a short time period.

Brian said he was too but now he had the conundrum on his hands.  He needed to find a way to get the IRS to understand the situation in a way that he could guide them to legally find out the same information without getting himself mired in quicksand.

He pointed out that Kekoa had followed a gift giving path to the wife of one judge in Indiana that seemed to have benefitted from a variety of very expensive gifts from Samuel.  She had a Lincoln and a diamond necklace gifted to her, that he had traced back to Samuel.  Then he had been able to trace some anonymous college tuition payments to the judge's two children.

He asked John and Hanna if they could handle getting the judge challenged about the gifts, he had received so that Samuel's gifts could go on record with the IRS.  Once that happened, he would be able to provide the information to the IRS that would lead them down the discovery trail to all the accounts that Samuel had at the various banks, and they could verify that he had not paid taxes on a huge financial income.

John said that he knew the person in charge at the IRS office and would give him a call.

## **<u>Chapter 10: The IRS</u>**

Joe was sitting at his desk reviewing an old money laundering case. He was the lead for the General Fraud and International investigation and Money Laundering, Non-filer Enforcement and Public Corruption Crimes unit. He had decided to reduce this ridiculously long title to Money Crimes Enforcement.

He had a team of specialists that helped him obtain and dig through information that was both on paper and in a variety of computer databases.

He had experienced many of the convoluted paths that schemers use to avoid taxes and hide their money. It had become a technological game of cat and mouse. He had no sympathy for individuals that chose willfully and intentionally not to comply with their legal responsibility to file required tax returns or pay their taxes.

His team had the investigators and the expertise critical to "following the money trail." Often the money trail led them into international waters. His team had successfully followed schemer's attempts to use foreign accounts, trusts, and other entities to commit criminal violations of the U.S. tax laws, and money laundering and Bank Secrecy Act (BSA) violations.

Many of those hiding their money in overseas accounts failed to submit tax returns on the money they believed to be out of sight and out of the reach of the IRS. He and his team prided themselves in making sure those individuals learned that the long arm of the IRS would get them.

His team covered a wide variety of public corruption investigations, a wide variety of criminal offenses including bribery, extortion, embezzlement, illegal kickbacks, entitlement and subsidy fraud, bank fraud, tax fraud, and money laundering. He and the team concentrated mostly on the tax and money laundering aspects of these investigations in cooperation with other federal, state, and local law enforcement agencies. His team's expertise had established their reputation as one of the leading groups in the fight against corrupt individuals and public officials.

He and the team had recently hit a dry spell in their work, and they were all reviewing previous cases to keep mentally sharp.

He was not prepared for the call that came in from one of his old college acquaintances about gifts being given to a judge in Indiana by a lawyer in Cincinnati.  The information he received stoked his curiosity.  He said he would take a quick look to see if his team needed to take any action.

He looked into the tax records of a lawyer, Samuel Herrington III.  The filed tax records indicated a lawyer barely breaking even.  He dug a little farther to see what his involvement was with the Indiana judge.  He found that the judge had handled a large number of cases for Samuel.  It seemed that ninety percent of the time the rulings went in favor of Samuel.

He looked up the judge's tax returns and found the normal judge's salary.

His radar went off when both the judge's and Samuel's tax returns seemed too squeaky clean.

There were no declared gifts or large declared expenses on returns going back for five years.

He had one of his agents go to the judge's courthouse to talk to the people working there.  He had another agent go and see about the judge's neighborhood, the parties he might have attended, the type of car that he or his wife drove and what the wife and the rest of the family did.

He was waiting for their reports when he was surprised by a call from Alex Evercrest who he was very much aware of because of her numerous news reports on the cases that she had solved.

She let him know that she had initiated an investigation of Samuel with a lawyer from Hawaii that had the goal of exposing billionaires that cheated in how they accumulated their wealth. She had asked him to look into Samuel's financial situation. This lawyer had surfaced the fact that Samuel had a variety of offshore bank accounts, under fictitious names, that in total had more than three billion dollars in them.

Joe almost fell out of his chair when he heard what she was telling him.

He asked why this lawyer had not come forward himself.

Alex replied that he had not obtained all his information in compliance with court standards but was willing to guide the IRS to all the locations and documents necessary to create an airtight case that would hold up in court.

Joe let her know that the amount of money they were talking about made him amenable to giving this lawyer legal protection for the information and he would also be in line for the top end reward percentage for recovering the taxes on an amount that she had mentioned.

Alex arranged a meeting for Brian and for his legal representative, John who would accompany him.

Joe asked if the John she was talking about was John Williams. She confirmed that it was.

He gave a small laugh and asked if there were any more surprises that she was going to surface on the call.

Alex replied that she had initialized the investigation, but she was not officially involved and was stepping away from the situation.  She added that she had also brought in John because the two of them had successfully won two cases against Samuel and that she knew that John had suggested putting the case in Joe's hands.

Joe thanked her for clarifying the circle he was stepping into and that he felt that everything could be worked out legally so that he could proceed with what seemed to be a clear case of someone purposely evading paying duly owed taxes.

After he hung up, he made a call to John to arrange for John, Brian, and him to meet.  He figured that would be the easiest way to get a clean working arrangement established.

Two days later, he greeted John and Brian as they were shown into his meeting room.

He was impressed when Brian introduced himself, briefly laid out his credentials as a lawyer so far licensed to practice law in Hawaii, California, and Washington State.  He listened as Brian explained that his goal was to identify and see that billionaires that defrauded, swindled, or deceived people or organizations in accumulating their wealth were brought to account.

He then listened to him explain that he had investigated John Herington III after Alex Evercrest had suggested that he do so.

Joe asked how Brian knew Alex and learned that he had met her at a party Alex threw at her house on Maui. The fact that Alex had a home in Maui was a surprise to Joe, but the link at least put things in context.

He then asked why Brian was in Cincinnati and learned about his romance with Annie Scots, a local artist that he was familiar with because of her being in the news a few years ago.

It was clear to Joe that the case he was about to undertake had a serendipity origin and that he was the one that would need to ensure that it would reach the court of law in a legally squeaky-clean shape.

He clarified that the information that Brian had surfaced was compromised as far as being presented in court.

Brian admitted that he could not present what he had without getting some sort of immunity agreement.

John suggested that the immunity agreement be drawn up and signed and then the detailed information that would lead to a rapid gathering of the information that would stand up in court could be planned.

Joe called in his support and asked her to get the paperwork typed up. He added that it should also call out for the reward compensation at the top level since it would be for a very substantial amount of money recovery.

While they waited, he asked Brian where his office was located and learned that he operated out of his home on Maui but would work on Joe's clock time during the upcoming investigation and would be available in person as the case might require.

He then asked how Brian had been able to obtain the information he was about to share and learned that Brian had hired a talented computer programmer that had been able to follow that trail and access the information.  He concluded that Brian had established a means of getting information that most sleuths would not be able to.

He commented that he was dying of curiosity and hoped his support would return soon.

John commented that it had been some time since the two of them had connected and that they should plan on a get together to share what they had been up to.

Just as they agreed on a get together time and place, the support came in with three copies of the requested paperwork.

Joe read the document to the three of them and asked if it was clear and acceptable.

John clarified that the thirty percent reward was on the amount of taxes that was paid for the money that was in the various bank accounts.

Joe verified that it was.

Brian then signed the documents that gave him protection and John signed as a witness and Joe put his signature at the bottom.

He then looked at Brian and asked if he was ready to share what he had.

Brian nodded and pulled his laptop out of his briefcase and asked how to hook up to the screen that was at the end of the table.

He took out a memory stick and plugged it into the computer and began.

He shared the locations of the banks, their routing numbers, and the account numbers where the money was held.  He even had the name and picture of the person at each bank that handled the account and the fake name that Samuel had used to establish it.

Joe gave a small whistle and asked how in the world Brian had been able to accumulate so much information and detail in such a short amount of time.

Brian smiled and said that his IT had been trained by the best and that he had used the latest technology to do so.  Then he had personally made the trip to each bank and used a picture of Samuel to verify that he was the person that had established each account.  The amount of money in each bank was obtained with the technology at hand.

Brian then commented that he was interested in making sure that Samuel would face the maximum penalty and that one strategy would be to charge him separately for the money being held in each bank.

John agreed that would allow the judge and jury to find Samuel guilty for three separate crimes.

Joe nodded and said that seemed like a good approach. He would discuss this with his team and decide on the details of how to proceed with them.

He then asked about the judge in Indiana.

Brian said that he had not dug as deeply into the judge, but he had discovered that the judge did have an offshore account and that his wife was the one that received the money and other very valuable gifts. So that case would need to be developed against a husband wife working together.

Joe asked whether Brian cared in which order he was to charge the judge or Samuel.

Brian shook his head and said that he did not and once he turned his information over to him, he would step aside and wait for him to initiate any additional involvement that might be needed. He then closed his file and pulled out his memory stick and handed it to Joe.

Joe thanked him and said that he would follow the trail and get all the information in a legal manner, organize it, and then make the charges.

He commented that the reward side of the agreement would potentially be years away and asked if that would be of any concern.

Brian shook his head and said that was not of any concern. He would be on to whatever came his way next and he would not be looking to this case except when Joe asked him to.

## **<u>Chapter 11: The Judge</u>**

Judge Singleton looked over the case that he was going to preside over.  It was what he called a Herrington case.  This meant that his wife would get a mysterious deposit from some unknown bank.  The amount always varied but was always substantial.  He preferred that the money was sent to the offshore account versus some of the gifts that she had received such as the Lincoln Black Label Navigator or the Raised Prong Miami Cuban Diamond Necklace.  Those gifts were too obvious even though they were given to his wife.

He had been doing this for enough years that he felt fairly safe in obliging Samuel in his request for leniency for his client or for throwing the case out of court.  He figured that most of the crimes were related to pushing a few drugs, though sometimes it was for a more serious crime for which he would give the lowest punishment possible.  He liked the fact that Samuel usually let him know the details of the case so that it was easy for him to decide what to do.  They made a point of never discussing the under the table compensation.

He had made sure that Samuel had the offshore back account and routing number and let him know that he preferred the gifts to go directly there.  His wife checked the account regularly and always knew what had been deposited.  For a total acquittal he charged two hundred thousand dollars.  The minimum for any situation was one hundred thousand dollars.  He and his wife had agreed that the offshore money was going to be untouched until he retired, and they moved to one of the Caribbean Islands.  He figured that would be a way to skip paying the taxes on an account that was enriched by an amount that he had no way of making on his salary.

He was surprised at the fact that Samuel got so many high paying clients.  It seemed that he had some sort of connection to the underworld.

The latest case was a simple one, but it was against a repeat offender, and he would need to give him some time.  He had indicated this to Samuel who had made the point that this person was the son of a rather high up drug boss that was willing to pay a little extra for the least amount of time possible.

He figured that he could make the time easier by putting this offender away in a minimum-security prison since he would be required to follow the sentencing guideline that specified the minimum sentence in his case.  This meant the length of penalty was set but the location was flexible.

# Hawaiian Phoenix

At the sentencing of this individual, the judge was surprised to learn that the defendant's father was in the courtroom. After the sentencing as the court was emptying, the father came up and thanked him. He quietly said that the briefcase in his office was a gift and that he should keep it and its contents.

As he walked down the hall to his office, he wondered what he was going to find.

When he got there his support pointed to a brown, hand tooled leather briefcase, with his name embossed in the leather and commented about what a nice briefcase it was. She said it had been dropped off with a note that said it was a gift from a grateful father. She handed him a sealed envelope with the keys to the briefcase and commented that she had looked up the briefcase brand and it was a very high-end brand.

He took the briefcase into his office and opened it to find bundled one-hundred-dollar bills. He locked his office door and pulled the bundles of money out and counted it. It was two hundred and fifty thousand dollars. A note thanked him for his consideration in how he handled the case.

He put the money back into the briefcase. He would need to have his wife spend the next several months moving the money through her bank account to the offshore account. He figured that his wife would figure out how to spend some of the money on some personal luxury items she was always talking about but that would be only a small portion of the money.

Brian had flown back to Maui so he could work with Kekoa on targeting the next billionaire. There was no hurry, but he wanted to develop a list of the top ten target billionaires. He figured that as they learned more about who these people were the list would flex and new names would be added.

Kekoa let him know that he had learned that the crooked judge's wife was transferring money from her account to their offshore account on a regular basis. She was keeping the amount below the threshold where it would trigger any questions. He added that he had been able to get into the Cincinnati bank where she first had to deposit the money before transfer and had obtained the serial numbers of the money that had so far been deposited.

Brian told him to send the information to Joe so that his team could follow up.

The next day, Joe admonished his team for not catching this fact and told them to go to the bank and see if they could get the serial numbers and find where the bills originated. He arranged to get a search warrant for the judge's home.

When the warrants were served and the search conducted, he was not surprised to learn that the wife had close to two hundred thousand dollars in a briefcase that had the judge's name on it. He figured it was time to make his first arrest and it would, by default, be the judge and his wife. He hoped that he could flip one of the two so that he could then arrest Samuel and bring him to justice.

Judge Singleton was reviewing a case when suddenly his door opened, and two men dressed in black suits and holding up their badges entered and declared he was under arrest for tax evasion.

He heard his secretary apologizing for not being able to stop the two.

He stood up and accepted the arrest warrant and quickly scanned it. He wondered how in the world they had found his offshore account.

His mobile phone rang, and he carefully removed it from his suit jacket and answered. It was Claire calling to let him know that two agents had given her paperwork that let them search the house and that they had found the briefcase with the money in their bedroom.

Leland knew then that he would not get to the Caribbean as soon as he had planned.

He put his hands in front of him as if to accept being handcuffed.

The two said that would not be necessary if he were willing to go with them to Cincinnati to be arraigned. They pointed out the alternative was to be put into a holding cell in his state and then be extradited to Cincinnati.

The judge agreed to go with them. He asked about Claire and learned that she would have the same option.

Leland asked to be able to call his wife. He asked where they would be housed while they awaited arraignment in Cincinnati and learned that the two would be put up in a hotel and would have an agent ensure they stayed in their room.

He called Claire and told her to pack their bags as if they were going for a several week vacation and then go with the agents and he would see her in Cincinnati.

He knew the maximum penalty for hiding the money and hoped that there would be enough left for the two of them to still be able to move to the Caribbean after they got out of prison.

He again wondered how he had been discovered. He figured it had something to do with Samuel and his practice of having money sent to the bank in the Caribbean.

He figured Samuel would be next. He wondered if Samuel had a clue about what was going on. He had no plans to shield him. In fact, if he was given the chance, he would work on getting a reduced sentence by implicating Samuel and give the names of those who had come before his court and been given lenient sentences in trade for the money that Samuel arranged.

Joe listened to the call that his agents made. He was pleased with the fact that they had the cash and that it was in a beautiful leather brief case with the Judges name embossed on it. He figured it could not get any better than that.

He would be able to get the bills traced.

He would have the judge's secretary's statement about the brief case.

He would send his agents to the associated banks to get the records of the Judge's and his wife's accounts history.  He was sure that he would be able to get the Caribbean bank to give him similar records and link both the wife and the Judge to that account.

The information he had from Brian indicated that the judge and his wife had almost reached the billionaire level, so he figured that the judge had been crooked for quite a while.  He would make sure that his team got all that information in a manner that it could be presented as evidence.

He thought about how he would link Brian as the source of the information so that he could get the reward for disclosing the situation.  He figured it represented a whopping forty million dollars.  He wondered what Brian would do with such a large sum.

He did not know it at the time that Brian was setting up a series of charitable organizations and also creating a list of existing charities that would receive the majority of the money.

He scheduled the interview of the judge and his wife for the following week.  He figured that once they came to court, he would need to be ready to move against Samuel.  He hoped that the judge and wife would agree to implicating Samuel.  If so, he would work on getting them the lowest penalty that they could get.

The following week he and several of his team members focused on the interview, organizing all the information, and getting prepared for the hearing where they would be charged. He also had to arrange for their defense.

The judge and the wife agreed to cooperate, and Joe was able to get the information that would allow him to arrest and charge Samuel.

Judge Singleton named the lawyer that he wanted to defend both he and his wife.

Joe had his team bring that lawyer up to speed. He figured that it was a clean case, and the defense would plead guilty and ask for leniency during the arraignment and the subsequent sentencing hearing.

He did not have any bias against a minimum sentence for the judge and his wife, but he had other thoughts about Samuel.

He also thought that Samuel was a flight risk. He assigned an agent to watch what Samuel was doing.

The act of having Samuel followed resulted in the agent identifying one of Cincinnati's top drug dealers meeting with him during several lunch sessions. The agent was able to capture some of the conversation and speculated that several of the dealer's pushers had been arrested and would be coming to trial. It seemed that a deal was being worked out that would move the trial to a venue outside of Cincinnati.

Joe knew that soon a call would be going out to Judge Singleton, and he needed to be ready at that moment to arrest Samuel.

## **Chapter 12: Samuel's Surprise**

Samuel looked at himself in the full-length mirror that was off to the side of his desk. He smiled as he thought about the success that he had in running his one-person law firm. He had five regular clients that each paid him one hundred thousand dollars a year retainer. These retainers were not on his "official" books but went directly into his offshore banks. He knew he was being paid in dirty money and used his accounts as a way to launder that money and made sure that the money traveled in a circle around his accounts and then a portion was returned to those retaining him. It was a simple arrangement that enriched him, and it served his clients as well.

He was being retained to represent people that had gotten in trouble with the law and to get them the best outcome possible when they went to court. The people retaining him were in top positions in various drug distribution rings.

Early on he had identified a judge interested in enriching himself and had set up an agreement with him to be rewarded for being lenient to his clients.  He would let the judge know what the offense was and whether the offender should receive a pass or if they should just get the minimum.

It was interesting to him that sometimes the drug boss did not want to pay for dismissal but only a minimum sentence.  At other times they would let him know that the offender should stand bare, by which they meant that the judge should just follow the legal guidelines.

He looked at the mirror again and smiled.  He had amassed a significant amount of money and was planning to shut his law practice down.

He had a one-hundred-acre estate, located on the east side of town, that had a six-bedroom two story stone façade exterior with a circular tower on one corner of the home located at the side of a large oval pond.

It was and was operated as a farm and provided him with every desired cut of meat, from beef, pork, lamb, to chicken and duck.  It also had greenhouses that produced a variety of vegetables.

As an operating farm it provided him with a significant tax break.

As he thought about a tax break, he smiled again and looked into the mirror and brushed back his hair.  He had paid no taxes on the money in the offshore accounts.  He figured he never would.  He thought of it as free money because the way he ran his books there was no indication it existed.  He never mixed any of his "official" office expenses with the money that was cash to the bank from some unknown source.  That money went through a rigorous and complex trip that when it was finally deposited looked like clean money to that bank receiving it.

He gave a little laugh as he looked at the circular diagram that he had created to show how honest and ethical he was.  In dark blue, serif typeface the title read, Circle of Best Legal Practices.  It had five circles.

Circle number one was labeled "Clear, Simple Billing practices."

Circle number two was labeled "Clear Fee agreement."

Circle number three was labeled "Ethical Billing."

Circle number four was labeled "Streamlined Time Keeping."

Circle number five was labeled 'Client focused, Easy agreement."

He had this diagram professionally rendered and had it in his office, his meeting room and at the entrance of his office behind his support's desk.

He indeed had simple billing practices.  He kept his billable hours to a minimum.  His fee agreements clearly stated that he made five hundred dollars an hour, but he only charged if his client was satisfied with the outcome of the verdict.  All paperwork in his office was designed to show how ethical he practiced his profession.  He had streamlined his time keeping by logging in each afternoon and documenting the case he was working on and the amount of time he had spent on it.  He laughed again as he thought about the fact that the amount of time was a complete fabrication.

The last circle stating that agreements were client focused and easy agreement was very true.  His clients were always pleased with the outcome that he ensured they would experience.  He purposely mixed legitimate cases with his underworld cases so that if he were audited his office would look like a well-managed honest practice.

Linda, his grandmotherly support, did all the grunt work of keeping the records.  He just made sure she had the information in a manner that would keep her clueless as to what was really going on.  When it came tax season, which happened every three months, she was the source of all the tax records and paperwork.  All he ever did was to sign off on what she and the tax accountant had agreed to.

On paper it looked like he was just getting by.  It also looked like he was a generous donor to a variety of local causes.

He was active in the upper echelon of the Cincinnati affluent, wealthy society.  At parties he was always on the lookout for his next fling.  He had affairs with numerous women and was surprised that he had a reputation among them for being super in bed.  He had almost married, but his wandering eye had moved on.  He was glad about that because it had allowed him to continue to enjoy the variety of bedroom ventures.

He decided to go for a walk to the river front to think about how he should set things up so that he would be able to access his offshore accounts.  He wanted to establish a home in the Caribbean, one in Asia or Australia and maybe one in South America.  He had considered Europe but was not sure about it.  Perhaps he would look into the Nordic region.  Denmark, Finland, Iceland, Norway, and Sweden had an attraction that he could not put his finger on, but he figured he would travel there and decide if he were interested in spending more time there.

He walked out to the reception area and let Linda know that he was going for a walk and then would most likely go home.

Almost immediately as he walked toward the park, he felt that he was being watched.  He had no clue who would be watching.  While he was waiting at a crosswalk to get clearance to cross, he carefully looked around.

He spotted one person, in a dark blue suit dutifully looking into a store window as if interested in the display and figured that since that person was looking into the window of a woman's dress shop, he must be the one following him. He purposely walked slowly on toward the park. The dark blue suit followed him.

He decided that he would call his primary underworld supporters to see if they had any inkling who might be interested in him. After making three calls it was clear to him that it was unlikely that the follower was connected to any of them.

The fourth call set off blaring alarm bells. He learned that Judge Singleton and his wife had been arrested and was currently in Cincinnati.

He looked over at where the dark blue suit was sitting on the park swings and knew that it was either the FBI or the IRS. He decided that it was time to get out of the country and he knew that he had to do it as soon as possible.

He walked slowly back to the parking garage and to his car. He noted that the blue suit followed him. He thought that he was going to make it but as he was getting ready to exit the garage, his car was blocked by a big black SUV and his car was surrounded by four men. They flashed their badges and let him know that he was being escorted to a meeting. He was ordered to get out of his car and taken into the SUV.

He asked about his car and was informed that it was being impounded and it would be searched. He could retrieve it later if things worked out.

He wondered what, "If things worked out" meant. He was expecting a trip to the courthouse or the jail house but instead they went to the IRS building in the heart of downtown. He was escorted into a meeting room and informed that he would soon learn the charges against him. He then realized that he had not been arrested and wondered what might be happening.

The person that came in introduced himself as Joe Brown, regional IRS unit leader. He had a set of legal looking papers that he put in front of him and then he looked across the table and said that he was holding the evidence that was going to put him away for fifteen to thirty years for, tax evasion, money laundering and association with several known organized crime groups. He would also face charges of bribing and paying off a judge.

Samuel was shocked. He wondered how the IRS could possibly have uncovered his well-designed scheme. It just seemed impossible to him. He commented that there must be some mistake and that he did not know what Joe was talking about.

Joe smiled and picked up one sheet and named the bank in Jamaica, the contact person there and the fictitious name he had used to set up that account. He held up two additional papers and said he had similar information for the other two banks.

He then held up two additional papers and said that they were the summary of the confessions of Judge Singleton and his wife that named him as the person who facilitated the money that went into their offshore account and for some other gifts that they had received.

Samuel said that unless he was under arrest he was going to leave.

Joe nodded and said that he should arrange for a lawyer because he would be arraigned the next day.  He then said that his home had been legally searched while he walked in the park and his legitimate passport and the illegitimate ones with the fictitious names, that he used to open up the offshore accounts had been confiscated.  He then pushed the final paper across the table and Samuel recognized it as a written version of the Miranda rights verbiage and heard Joe putting him under arrest.

Two uniformed police entered and put him in hand cuffs as they read him his rights as well.  This time he was escorted out and taken to the jailhouse that was across the street from the courthouse.

He made his one phone call to a lawyer that he had previously used in one of his legal cases and got him to represent him and to be present the next day in court.

He spent an uncomfortable night, unable to sleep as he thought through how he would handle the situation.  It seemed that the Judge had pointed the finger but how had Joe been able to make the leap from that to find the three banks that he used.

That seemed to be an impossible leap.  The judge might have been able to point a finger at him for bribing him but there was no way the judge had any idea about the rest.

Something just did not seem quite right.

Samuel was on the right track, but he had no idea about the fact that he would never learn how the leap had occurred.

130

## **Chapter 13: Unwilling**

Linda looked up from her desk at two men in matching dark blue suits, as they walked in, removed their dark sunglasses, and walked briskly to her desk.  One of them pulled out some papers and told her he had a search warrant to search and seize all information that she and Samuel Herrington III had.  She took the paper and quickly read the opening paragraph and then looked at the signature and the notary witness seal.  She looked up at the two men and asked to see their badges.  After verifying that they were from the IRS she asked what she was supposed to do.

One of them used his phone and suddenly the room filled with a group of people that went into Samuel's office and not long after began to take out boxes filled with his files.  His computer and monitor were carried out as well.

She asked what her boss had done to have the IRS descend on the office and take its contents.  She was surprised to learn that he was being charged with money laundering, bribing a judge and with not paying taxes on a large amount of money that was currently in offshore banks.

She asked if she was under arrest.

The person that had presented the search warrant shook his head and said that at this point she was not being arrested or detained.  She was free to stay or leave.

A person came out of Samuel's office and asked if she knew the combination to the safe.

She shook her head and said she had no clue about the safe or the combination for it since she did not know that Samuel had a safe.

She pointed to her filing cabinets that had been emptied and made the point that they each were fireproof and were locked up like a safe and she had the combination to them.  She commented that those files were all legitimate and they were organized in an efficient manner.

She went to her desk and pulled out a paper that defined how the files were organized and handed it to the agent that had given her the search warrant and told him that the diagram was the layout of the files she had on her computer and for the folders in the hanging files.  She added that if they followed the diagram, the work of looking through her information would go much faster.

She then made the point that they would find that her information was clear, well organized and accounted for all the money that moved through the practice and her office and that it was as far as she knew all legitimate, legal and that the taxes had been paid.  She added that as far as she knew all the transactions, she had recorded were legitimate and accounted for.

She then volunteered that she, the business lawyer, and the accountant all worked together to make sure that the finances were legally managed and clearly documented.

She sat down at her desk and called up three documents and printed them out.  One was the normal monthly financial statement, one called out the cases that were being charged and the last was a document that granted her a bonus for the year.  She quickly typed up another document that paid her full salary for the rest of the year.

She made copies and handed a copy to the lead IRS agent and asked if she could get Samuel's signature on the documents.

He looked through the document and commented that he hoped she could get the signatures on all of them.  He smiled at her and said that the two that affected her would most likely be some of the last money that her boss would be spending.  The rest would most likely be spent on legal fees to pay for his defending lawyer.

He told her that Samuel was being held in the county holding jail.

She asked if she could get that day in to have him sign the papers.

He made a call and then told her that she would be able to go to the county jail and Samuel would be escorted to the meeting room.

She thanked him and asked if she would be able to get back into the office in the morning.

He shook his head and said that office would be designated as a crime scene and taped off.  Once all the materials of interest were removed then perhaps the office could be reopened.

Linda decided to get the paperwork signed, go to the bank, move the money that represented her pay to the end of the year and a bonus for her outstanding services to her personal bank account, and then go out to dinner.  She figured that she would be looking for a job or maybe she thought it was time for her to retire.

She walked from the office to the jail and once there she was able to enter and was led to a meeting room.  A few moments later Samuel was escorted in by two officers and shackled to the table.

Linda commented that she was sorry to see him in an orange overall and that he had not been able to dress in his normal sleek, good-looking clothes.

Samuel smiled and asked if his office was still in one piece.

Linda let him know that his office had been emptied of most of his records and that his safe had been found.

He nodded and let her know that he had given the IRS the combination to the safe.

Linda handed him the papers she had brought with her and handed him a pen.  She asked him to read them and then sign them if he agreed.

She watched him smile and nod when he got to the one that paid her through the end of the year and was relieved that he signed it.  Then he surprised her by modifying the one giving her a bonus and commented that he was increasing her bonus.  She saw him changing it by adding one in front of the fifty thousand, initial the change and then he had the two officers sign as witnesses to the change.

Samuel looked at her and asked her to continue to run his office until after his trial.  He asked her to contact all the clients he had and to put them in contact with five lawyers whose names he wrote down.

It was clear to her that his ego had taken a hit.  She commented that he made the orange jump suit appear fashionable.

He smiled and said that he appreciated her keen eye and that he was now going to his new office and think about how to make his way out of the jail cell.

Linda decided that the best course of action was to first go to the bank and move the money that was coming to her into her bank account.  She would then go to her financial analsyist and put that money into the appropriate accounts.

She decided that after that she would celebrate by enjoying a good lunch and then go to the bookstore.  She figured that she would have plenty of free time in the coming weeks and decided to stop at a bookstore and select books that she would read in the coming weeks.  As she ate lunch, she decided that a good travel guide would be one of the books she would be looking for.

## **<u>Chapter 14: Next</u>**

It seemed to Brian that he had spent most of the year flying back and forth between Maui and Cincinnati.  He knew many of the flight attendants on an almost personal level.  Annie had been great about how she handled his travels and had returned with him several times.  She had looked into schools for the girls and had them enrolled in the one that they had chosen.  She let him know that they were eager to make the move at the end of the school year.

The trials of the judge and his wife was shortened because they both pleaded guilty and went straight into being sentenced. They had made a deal with the IRS to provide information on a long list of bribes that they had received from Samuel and in exchange the prosecution had recommended that the judge be lenient and had recommended a minimum-security prison.  The judge found both of them guilty of a series of charges that he detailed but after announcing his verdicts, he ran the sentences concurrently.  He then sent them both to the same prison.

Brian was surprised at the leniency but figured they would still be incarcerated for three years.  The fact that they would still have a very significant amount of money after their release did not escape him.

He was surprised by the monetary reward amount that he received for the information he had provided.  It represented a three hundred percent increase in his personal wealth.

Samuel's trials went on for a much longer period of time and they were more complicated in that he had amassed a much larger amount of money in a very complicated money laundering scheme, and he was also being charged with tax evasion.  He faced a much longer period of time in jail.

His lawyers had won a request that the two major charges be tried separately.  They were trying to make a deal to pay the taxes and have that charge reduced to the penalty of paying the taxes late and being made to pay the late charge.

They were granted that request.

That settlement led to Brian getting a reward that was triple the settlement that he had received from the judge's and wife's settlement.

He was called to testify that he had been the one that followed a hunch that led to his discovery of Samuel's accounts when he had discovered Judge Singleton's account.  That same bank had identified a picture of Samuel as one of their other clients.

The money laundering charge was one that, given the manipulation route the money followed during laundering, was much harder to deny and to get a softer judgement on. The jury seemed to grasp the fact that it was purposely perpetrated, and they seemed inclined to side with the prosecution more than with the arguments that the defense made.

Brian thought that the prosecution presented a very detailed, easily understood, make sense, way of moving the money from one bank to another in a variety of directions and amounts as it was laundered. They used a large diagram to show how that occurred. He understood that it was more complex than presented but it provided the basic information in laymen's terms.

Samuel was found guilty of the money laundering scheme and sentenced separately for the money that each bank had in his account and his sentences would run sequentially. He faced a total of fifteen years in prison.

Brian received his reward for the amount held in each bank. This amount put him embarrassingly close to being a billionaire when added to all the other rewards he had received.

He decided it was time to set up several of his charities and to give several established charities substantial amounts of money. He engaged a trust fund management group to provide professional guidance and to do it in such a manner that it reduced his personal tax exposure.

He and Kekoa spent time in going through the list of potential next billionaires that they should pursue.  It was a surprise to both of them at how long the list of questionable billionaires was completed and they were more surprised when the name of the most probable billionaire surfaced.

**_The End_**

## About the Author

Ronald E.  Mueller
remwriter95@gmail.com

Ron grew up in what is now Flint River State Park in Southeast Iowa.  The 170-year-old house Ron lived in is built into a hillside.  It faces a 125-foot-high cliff towering over the little Flint River.  The house and the land talked to him about; the passing of time, the struggle to conquer the land, the struggles people faced and the wonder of nature.

He climbed the cliffs, crawled into the caves, dove from the swimming rock, collected clams from the bottom of the pond, gigged and skinned frogs for their legs.  He trapped muskrats for fur, hunted raccoons in the dead of night, and with only a stick hunted rabbits in the dead of winter.

His young life was outdoors, and nature tested him.

He walked to a one room stone schoolhouse uphill both ways.  A stern but warm-hearted teacher, Mrs. Henry was instrumental in shaping his character as she shepherded him from the fourth to the eighth grade.  She ran a Montessori before its time.  It was a great way to grow up.

His experiences inter-twined with snippets of fantasy lend themselves to the adventures he leads the reader through.

Ron Mueller



Published by: Around the World Publishing LLC.

QR Links to
ATWP.US web site